THE
ECHOING

THE
ECHOING

A NOVEL

JESSICA BLACKBURN

BONNEVILLE
BOOKS

An imprint of Cedar Fort, Inc.
Springville, Utah

ISBN 13: 978-1-4621-1894-6

Published by Bonneville Books, an imprint of Cedar Fort, Inc.
2373 W. 700 S., Springville, UT 84663
Distributed by Cedar Fort, Inc. www.cedarfort.com

Library of Congress Cataloging-in-Publication data on file

Cover design by Rebecca J. Greenwood
Oneonta Gorge photography by Andrew Coelho via unsplash.com
Cover design © 2016 Cedar Fort, Inc.
Edited and typeset by Justin Greer

Printed in the United States of America

10 9 8 7 6 5 4 3 2 1

Printed on acid-free paper

PRAISE FOR JESSICA BLACKBURN AND *THE ECHOING*

"An incredible debut by Jessica Blackburn! *The Echoing* is a powerful story with beautiful emotional threads that will stay with you long after you've reached the end. With raw depth of feeling and captivating excitement, Blackburn brings to life a moving story of strength and sacrifice that is sure to satisfy YA readers' hearts."
–Amber Lynn Perry, author of the *Daughters of His Kingdom* series

"Jessica Blackburn's debut novel, *The Echoing*, is a spellbinding teenage story about discovery, friendship, gifts, and twists of fate. What starts out as a story about Rylee rediscovering her crush with childhood friend, Merritt, soon tilts and spins into a plot surrounded by a gift that can transform events. The unsettling familiar emotion of the blind recluse woman deep in the woods, who calls Rylee the balancer, spooks and startles her, the old lady's words haunting Rylee long after she is within the safety of her own home again. Their first encounter is not their last, as beginnings become endings, and endings offer answers to beginnings. Rylee soon unearths clues from the old woman and feels opposition in the hypnotic evil power of Nathaniel, all the while becoming closer to Merritt as she navigates the unknown."
–Amy Jo Wilde, author of *White Bees*

"*The Echoing* by Jessica Blackburn is a must read for teens to adults! The author does such a great job in bringing the main character, Rylee, to life, leaving you with the desire to read more and more! As you get to know this sarcastic and honest girl, you won't be able to put the book down as you get captured away into her curious life. This book is only the start of a wonderful beginning for Jessica and I am so excited for the world to experience *The Echoing*."
–Danielle Davis, owner & creator of *Today's the Best Day*

"Jessica Blackburn brings ancient mythology to modern-day experience in a captivating, heart-expanding hero's journey that young adults will be sure to adore and return to again and again. Through the emerging heroine Rylee, readers wrestle with questions that have plagued humanity since Adam and Eve partook of the fruit—how come bad things happen to good people? What is the point of sorrow? of joy? The range of all humanity's emotional experiences? The journey to discover those answers, through mystical encounters, high school lunches, world religion classes, and more, will keep you reading through the night and neglecting chores and sit-down meals. Consider this a warning!"
–Tara Boyce, editor and writer

For my husband, Mitchell.
You are my everything.

Prologue

As time birthed into beginning, the bewitching serpent whispered its cunning words to Eve, persuading, "Partake of the forbidden fruit and ye shall be as God, knowing good and evil."

And so Eve fell.

The battle of opposition must blossom inside every living soul. We know without sin, there is no righteousness. And without the existence of righteousness there could be no happiness, nor punishment, nor misery. And if these things are not, we are not as well.

Without the forbidden act of transgression, Eve and Adam would never have fallen but would have remained confined to the Garden of Eden. And all things that were created must have lingered in the same state forever and had no end. A state of innocence: having no joy, for they could taste no misery.

> *"Adam fell that men might be; and men are,*
> *that they might have joy."*
> 2 Nephi 2:25

Chapter 1

No woe or despair of absolute misery could compare to the torment of sitting through the daily morning announcements. My mind gradually rotted away as I leaned on my desk listening to Principal O'Connors drag on about the severe problems of the cafeteria's unrecycled soda bottles. His monotone voice trickled through the speakers and cast a slumbering spell over all the residing students of homeroom class.

The potato masher of boredom squashed my wasted brain cells as my heavy eyelids painted in smoky shadows of grey kept closing, persuading me to fall asleep. Every time I caught myself nodding off I would readjust my sitting position, taking in deep breaths to refresh my decaying energy.

I attempted to distract myself by pulling back my choppy hair into a messy ponytail. My dark bangs slipped through the grip of the elastic headband, so I pulled out a loose bobby pin and sculpted them up into a towering bump on top of my head.

Mr. O'Connors concluded his remarks like a lifeless turtle, "Thank you, Bulldogs, for listening to your morning announcements, and good day." Click. Click. Click.

We listened with amusement as the microphone shuffled over the intercom. Students snickered as he endeavored to disconnect the audio. "No, Betty, it's still on. Why won't it—" CLICK.

I twisted to glance out the classroom window, catching a glimpse of a giant red barge floating down the river in the distance. The town of Stevenson resided on a steep hillside along the Columbia, separating the Oregon and Washington border. To the south, one could always see the massive flowing river and tree-covered hillsides of the other shore.

Railroad tracks stretched out along the rim of town and were constantly accompanied by cargo trains casually passing through. The sounds of train whistles and chattering tracks became white noise to the local residents.

Everyone in the nestled community carried a neighborly charm, making it nearly impossible to avoid the overzealous, little-town friendliness that attacked you from every angle. Your bank teller, your barber, your dentist, and your kindergarten teacher, who somehow still remembers that amusing day when you dropped your macaroni all over the teeter-totters, skip around the local shops seeking you out to yap your ear off.

Surrounding the town was a thick wilderness of back country. Bulges of hillsides stood out above the towering trees, and miles and miles of streams and waterfalls sprinkled the countryside.

Stevenson's modest population allowed the residents only one high school, small enough to fill the entire student class in seven crinkled yearbook pages. Though I walked these halls every day, it felt like a distant part of my life. I had no attachment or welcoming feelings associated with the school doors I entered daily.

There was some sort of glitch of emptiness attached to

my role in the environment. A faint whisper deep inside of me always reminded me that I didn't quite belong. Whether it meant I was destined for greater things or perhaps that I wasn't meant to be at all, I felt my life had a missing puzzle piece waiting to be discovered.

I bounced like a pinball from class to class and before I knew it, the school day was almost half over. Classes still hadn't become too great of a challenge yet. Homework and assignments usually began to pick up dramatically by the end of September, but right now, everyone was still getting back into the swing of the new school year.

Shyler walked beside me toward the lunch hall. Her short blond hair prickled out framing the outline of her smooth, angelic face. The silver bracelets that dangled from her wrists chimed together like sweet bells as her arms swayed freely with each step.

It was difficult for me to find friends I was patient enough to put up with. Most people were too ridiculous to be around. Everyone seemed to share the same shallow, conforming traits and molded together desperately longing for acceptance. But Shyler was unique.

As I thought about it, I realized we were completely opposite in almost every way. It was similar to an odd friendship between a cool-headed peacock and an inattentive milk goat. She had a confidence in herself with no fear of showing it. Yet I was drifting without a conscious identity to claim for myself, silently staring out in the distance with a crooked mouth stuffed with tasteless grass. Like a magnet, our differences were what linked us closely together.

"So, this scholarship program I was telling you about earlier, for the Kenneth Adams Foundation," Shyler spoke with her mouth full of food. "I should have my application complete by the end of this week. Did you get a chance to look at the link I sent you?"

I poked my cafeteria noodles with a flimsy, plastic fork and sighed. "I've been busy. Isn't it a little early to worry about scholarships? Sophomores don't graduate for another two years."

"Not me," she said, cheerfully. Her expression oozed out with excitement as she brought up the good news. "If I get all my advanced classes out of the way, the school counselor thinks I'll meet the requirements to graduate as a junior!"

My heart became heavy. Sourly scanning the room, I studied my fellow classmates. If Shyler left me a year early, there wouldn't be anyone else around delightful enough to share a conversation with. The thought of surrounding myself with any of my other peers seemed more unpleasant than swallowing my own vomit.

"I guess I hadn't thought that far ahead yet," I said with disappointment.

"You really haven't thought about it? I mean, there's a whole world out there waiting for us to influence and we won't make much progress being stuck in a small town like this! Don't you ever feel like you were meant for bigger things?"

Her question caused a fluttering inside my chest. I pondered her words intensely, attempting to translate my inner emotions about my self-fulfilling purpose. Yes, deep inside, I thought I was meant for something bigger, but I couldn't explain it or understand exactly what it was my soul was aching to discover. It felt so familiar, yet, so unanswered, like the aftertaste of déjà vu. In my mind, my fingers reached out for the evidence of what it meant, trying to nudge something mystical and instead touched more of a liquid matter than the solid texture it so curiously desired.

I had this feeling soaking inside my soul that echoed to me repeatedly, "You'll find it someday. It is your destiny." Whatever it was, I hadn't discovered it yet, but I knew there was more to me than I understood.

As Shyler multitasked, devouring her food and studying her excessive class notes, I glanced toward the corner of the cafeteria where a quiet girl sat alone against the wall and ate her lunch on the floor. She wore baggy clothes that hung in a tasteless position, unable to flatter her skinny form. Her dyed hair had a wavy crease that circled awkwardly around the sides of her face.

Entering from the same corner of the lunchroom, a group of immature boys thundered their way inside. By their variety of lopsided hats, head-scarves, and low rider jeans, it was easy to translate the unspoken message that they took great pleasure in creating trouble. One boy stood out in particular with nasty patches of half-grown facial hair giving off the vibes of one demanding fear and respect. My eyes dropped down to his swollen fingers with double studs pierced into the skin between each knuckle.

As he spotted the lonely girl, he quickly ran ahead of the group and kicked the corner of her lunch plate, sending her meal flying in every direction across the floor. Milk dripped down the front of her oversized shirt and puddled into her lap.

The gang of boys laughed and continued stepping on the mess of food, crunching the crumbs into smaller and smaller pieces. The girl shrank back into the corner and stared directly at the ground to avoid eye contact as they continued to pass by.

Inside of me I felt sorry for her being mercilessly picked on. I watched her light colored eyebrows narrow intensely to fight back tears of embarrassment as she wiped the milk from her clothes. My sorrow quickly transitioned to anger toward the bullies who had humiliated her. They continued walking away, completely unaware of the deep pain that lingered in their trail of cruel actions.

I sat silently in my chair. There was nothing I would do to stand up for her. I wasn't exactly the hero-type who skipped around the school in a bright red cape and leotards seeking justice for my poorly treated peers, but in my heart I desired for the wrong to be made right from a distance. It stirred and spread inside me like a wildfire.

"Maybe I should go to law school," I said to Shyler, without looking away from the group of heartless boys. "I think I'd enjoy watching criminals being punished for their actions." I turned to Shyler with a fake smile plastered across my face.

"*You*? Standing up in the courtroom in front of an audience of people *by choice*?" Shyler snickered, trying to avoid choking on her food. "Good one, Rylee."

"Yeah, I guess that's not really my style," I agreed. I turned again to the corner of the room. The skinny girl waited until she was alone and slowly inched away from her seat, picking up little bits and pieces of food and setting them back on her plate.

She looked up in my direction for a brief moment, and our eyes met. I quickly glanced away to save her from embarrassment and probably to save myself too, since I had witnessed her troubles and had sat back doing nothing.

The class bell rang.

"All right, ladies, don't forget Friday we're having solo auditions. Anyone who wants to try out, make sure you're practicing!" Mr. Luke tried to speak above the chatter of garrulous girls as they grabbed their school bags and filed out of the choir room.

"He might as well give me the solo now and save

everyone the disappointment of being let down," Addison announced, as she walked away with her posse of friends.

Her hair of beach blond highlights was always perfectly sculpted. Everywhere she walked, she left a trail scented of vanilla and brown sugar. The extra three inches of height from her heeled boots made her tower above her peers, conveniently allowing her lifted button nose to raise even higher in the air.

"And *anyone* can try out, Addison," Mr. Luke reaffirmed as she strolled away. I casually pulled out my textbooks from under my chair and waited for the congested crowd to die down before following outside.

"Have a good day, Rylee," Mr. Luke said without looking up from his desk. The deep sound waves of his voice glided softly through the empty room. "You should consider trying out this Friday."

"Ha. Thanks, Mr. Luke. I'll think about it."

Not likely. Anything involving the center of attention I eagerly avoided. It's not that I was bashful or had problems being outgoing, I just preferred sitting back and watching others take the stage.

I enjoyed being taught, being inspired, but most of all, being humored by people making fools of themselves. Some individuals had zero-problems jumping up and displaying to the world their character of quirks and flaws. I was a comfortable wallflower and had no stirring desire to "take the lead" in any situation.

When I left the choir room, the hallway became desolate as students scrambled to their next destinations. I walked past the bright yellow walls plastered with student council posters and adorned with black and white sports team pictures, plaques, and dusty trophies.

As I turned the corner, I was startled with the sudden greeting of Merritt Emerson.

"Well, if it isn't Rylee Perry!" He grinned with a half smile as he spoke. He was leaning back against a row of paint-chipped, red lockers, waiting for a nearby classroom to open. The ends of his thick, brown hair always seemed to curl up underneath his brimmed beanie. His dark brown eyes sparkled and immediately caught my undivided attention. It made it nearly impossible to concentrate. "How was your summer?"

As kids, the two of us were almost inseparable. We would spend every hour of our summertime outside exploring and building tree forts until the sun fell down behind the peaks of the mountains. He was two grades ahead of me, so once he started middle school our daily walks from the bus stop and early years of friendship inevitably came to an end.

The fact that Merritt was choosing to acknowledge me right now was slightly shocking. Not that he was the conceited type who would brush me off; it was just rare that our paths ever crossed anymore. I welcomed the attention with enthusiasm.

"My summer was ridiculously awesome. I don't even know where to start," I answered back.

"Really?" he asked.

"Yeah—no. Not really. I was working the coffee shop most of the time."

He grinned and looked down at the car keys dangling in his hand beside his soda bottle. Standing beside him now, I realized he had become much taller than I remembered. As hard as I tried to look away, my vision was cemented to his distinctive face. The smile lines etched into his cheeks seemed as if they were perfectly chiseled by an ivory sculptor.

"How was yours?" I asked back, politely.

"I was gone for most of it," he replied. "We did a lot of traveling."

"That's right, your mom took you and your sister to Europe? I think my dad was taking care of your mail while you guys were gone." Realizing how stalker-like I sounded, I quickly stopped talking. I knew way too many details about his personal life for someone who never spoke to him anymore, but he seemed to brush it off like he didn't notice.

The ringing of the second bell hammered through the building and I knew he needed to get to class.

"I better go, Ry, but we should catch up sometime. It's been too long. Good to see you," he said.

"You too, Merritt. I'll see you around."

I wished he didn't have to go, but I held onto his words that assured me we would speak again. It felt so wonderful to be able to run into an old friend.

For the rest of the school day, I attempted to concentrate but found my mind wandering off to memories with Merritt, playing together as kids in our backyard hills of unexplored wildernesses.

Chapter 2

I said SOY MILK! Is it really too much to ask for in a latte? What's wrong with you people today?!"

Ah, Mr. Kestler. The barista staff was graced with his affable presence at the beginning of every week.

"I am so sorry," I apologized. "We will get you a new drink immediately." Snatching the cup from his hand, I poured the unwanted beverage down the sink.

Most of my afternoons working the coffee shop were pleasant, but I was never a fan of Mondays when Mr. K showed up in his bright red Corvette.

He worked as some fancy financial advisor always making his traditional stop for coffee along his weekly commute. It was nearly impossible to get his order right. Even when I did, he would find something else to complain about.

"And these cinnamon rolls . . . No one explained to me that there were raisins inside!"

His thin, slicked back hair leeched tightly to the sides of his round skull. Like a paint-splattered canvas, his dark freckles overpopulated his skin and claimed two thirds of his facial surface.

"So sorry, Mr. Kestler. We ran out of plain rolls this

morning. Would you like a bagel instead?" I asked like a composed preschool teacher would approach a child to solve a trivial conflict.

"No, I would not like a bagel. I would like a cinnamon roll with NO RAISINS!" he snapped back. "And if there's nothing you can do to fix that, then perhaps I'll take my business elsewhere."

If only, Mr. K. If only.

I came home to find the house in utter chaos. Dad and a few friends from work were watching baseball in the living room, jumping from their seats and yelling at the buzzing TV screen.

A forced puff of air passed my lips in irritation as I came through the entryway. Dad lived and breathed baseball and had failed to pass on the passion to me. He had played back in college before I was born and still loved to find any excuse to toss a ball around. I understood why it meant so much to him. Unfortunately, it wasn't enough to appreciate being surrounded by enclosed walls of screaming grown men. No matter what room I tried to hide myself in I couldn't escape the synchronized hollers and cheers coming from the sports den.

The stairs were adorned with my brother's plastic race cars and towers of building blocks. Finding a safe pathway to the top was like creeping through a dangerous minefield.

As I climbed the steps, the edge of my heel barely skimmed the corner of a sharp block causing the reflexes in my right leg to go limp to avoid putting weigh on it. I started tipping sideways and flung my arms out against the rail and the wall to catch my balance. I laughed at how awkward I looked as I stumbled my way up the remaining steps.

"Harrison, are you trying to kill me?! I swear I'll throw your toys in the river!" I shouted, hoping he was somewhere nearby to hear to my livid threat.

I felt a quick pop lightly hit the back of my head. When I turned around, Harrison stood shirtless pointing a foam-dart gun directly at my face. He giggled and peeked up from under his oversized cowboy hat, then took off running in the other direction. For as small as he was, I couldn't deny that the kid was incredibly quick and sly.

Upstairs, Mom had her personal office space turned upside-down as she worked on her latest painting project. She was a tidy person on the average day, but once creativity seized her, nothing could get in the way of her art. Cluttered materials could wait to be cleaned and messy piles were put on hold so nothing could stop her imagination from spiraling.

I watched her eyes behind her thick-rimmed glasses study the movements of her paintbrush as it glided the mixing colors across the white canvas. All of her artwork had a dreamlike signature that carried me away into an intriguing state of limbo. The masterpieces felt like gateways to other worlds, and eyes of unearthly investigators curiously stared back through my mom's self-created windows.

"Hey, Ry-Ry. How was school today?" Her focus never shifted as she delicately pushed back a loose strand of brunette hair behind her ear, avoiding the sticky paint that caked her fingertips.

"Fine. Do you know how long the guys will be downstairs?" I asked, impatiently.

Just then I heard a roaring rampage thunder beneath the floor.

"No!"

"Boo!"

"C'mon, ump! What kind of call was that?"

Mom laughed. "I wouldn't count on them leaving anytime soon."

I sighed and knew trying to study in the house would be completely pointless. Along with Dad's love for baseball, I also lacked Mom's skills of concentrating on her work while shutting out nearby distractions.

" 'Kay, I'm going for a walk then." I patted the wooded doorway frame and spun around.

"Dinner's at seven tonight! Harrison has karate so it'll be a bit late," Mom called out as I tiptoed back downstairs, glaring at the scattered toys that continued to threaten my balance.

Harrison was a fireball of energy. Mom signed him up for karate along with his active preschool class to assist him in channeling out his bubbling zeal of activity. It felt like he could run circles around all of us for days without rest.

I grabbed my coat draped over a kitchen chair before opening the back door. Following closely behind me was our dog, Beck, trying to escape the cacophony of noise and Harrison's target practice.

My shoes crunched on the rocky pavement as we pushed up the hillside. Beck's nose stayed glued to the ground while she roamed back and forth smelling every crack and crevasse that bordered the trail. Her white tipped tail bounced in the air as she zigzagged through the trees. She was supposedly a mutt-mix with her short hair sprinkled in every color of spots imaginable, but based on her pattern of sniffing everything in her path, I always suspected a majority of hound in her bloodline.

The overcast of clouds glazed the scenery with a whitish-gray coat. Even though it was deep cold, the crisp brightness was pleasant. My lungs welcomed the chilling air, and my eyes watered as the breeze brushed lightly past my face.

Living outside of town had its share of exceptional

perks. Two acres past our driveway marked the beginning of miles and miles of untouched wilderness. Growing up on the edge of the forest, these trees had accompanied my imagination on childhood journeys across pirate-infested waters, through secret channels of dragon caves, and along countless battles against ferocious sasquatch-armies.

Brodie Mitchell, an old classmate from elementary days, claimed seeing Sasquatch in these woods years ago. About five miles north of town he was out searching for hidden caches. All of the sudden one stumbled out from behind a thick bush, turned and stared Brodie right between the eyes, then sprinted away. He said its animal movement seemed uncommonly quick and agile compared to the clumsy "Bigfoot" stereotype he had always imagined. Everyone told him he had mistaken it for a frightened black bear, but to this day he boldly refused to deny his story.

On my usual evening walks, I traveled parallel to a hidden stream that eventually led me down a red dirt road a half a mile from home, but today I wanted to get away. My body was in the mood for a change of scenery and physical activity. I looked up to the tall, inviting treetops heading west and whistled for Beck who was preoccupied with her nose planted in a nearby hole small enough for a ground squirrel.

As my leg muscles burned on the steep slope I continued pushing farther and farther away from my well-known environment. Once we reached the top of the hill, I scanned the unfamiliar surroundings. Through the thick trees I spotted an old, dark shack standing alone. The dirty boards and rusty roof were falling apart, and the frail sides were covered with growing thorn bushes and black tree moss. The sight of the hut caught me off guard, and I immediately froze.

Something seemed eerie and out of place in my newly

stumbled-upon location. All of the nearby plants and trees looked withered and dead, as if the atmosphere alone had cut off their life supply. Dry branches hung low while the neighboring shrubbery shadowed in a mixture of dull coloring.

Beck's head shot up immediately. As her ears and tail rose upward, a growling rumble stirred in the back of her throat.

A strange feeling quickly overwhelmed me. The emotion was so unfamiliar that I couldn't determine if my senses were trying to warn me of danger or draw me towards the foreign habitat.

This little hut felt familiar; like I had seen it in a forgotten dream or perhaps had felt its loneliness as it weakly trembled to hold the weight of the roof it so desperately longed to detach from.

I jumped as Beck howled intensely. Before I was given a chance to react, she was bolting straight toward the shelter.

"Beck, no!" I screamed. "Come back!"

The aggressive behavior was completely outside of her normal, timid character. She rushed around the perimeter of the structure and with a quick pivot, crouched down and faced the doorway. Her tail fell directly between her legs and her sharp teeth flashed through the slits of her mouth. Even from a distance I could see her black and white hairs sticking up behind her neck.

Suddenly, I heard rustling come from the inside of the shack, almost like a hissing or a whispering. But from my angle there was no way to see the source of the mysterious noise.

My breathing stopped, and my heart began pounding harder. I felt my cheeks flush red as I finally translated the emotion I had been experiencing moments earlier. *Danger. Danger is the feeling you're sensing, stupid.*

Beck slowly shuffled backwards, kicking up dust as she barked ferociously. My instincts tussled in the back of my brain, begging me to turn back and sprint away, but I couldn't leave Beck, knowing something else was there that could harm her.

The airy cry coming from inside the doorway began growing louder. Without much thought -scratch that, there was no logical thinking involved- my legs took off and carried me in the direction of Beck and the front door. I had to get to my dog and face whatever lay guarding the shack.

As I raced around to the front of the shelter, I was startled by the unexpected scene that awaited me in the doorway. My eyes pierced through the darkness, spotting an elderly woman hunched down in the shadows.

Ratted and gray, her long braids of tangled hair rested low on each shoulder. Her weathered skin stretched across her scarred face. And her eyes, the smoky gloss that wrapped over her large pupils gave the impression that she must have been mostly, if not entirely, blind.

My stomach churned as I watched her, crouched down, rocking back and forth in the darkness. I was terrified by her strange behavior as she muttered to herself under her breath.

By the growing tone in her voice, I detected that Beck's barking was clearly aggravating her. Paralyzed with shock, I stretched out to the bottom of my soul, reaching for any shred of courage. Somehow I managed to choke out the words, "Are you all right?"

The woman went silent and still. To swallow my fear, I tried to see past her frightening appearance. Perhaps she was struggling and in need of aid. I reached down, trying to calm Beck and stop her from barking.

"I'm sorry about my dog," I apologized. "She's just not used to seeing strangers out here. Normally, she's quite friendly. Can I help you with anything?" I asked, timidly.

Her neck jerked immediately to the side and her piercing eyes filled my heart with terror; crushing me with an enormous weight. Although I didn't think I was incredibly visible, I felt like she saw straight into me. It was as if she knew my past, my future, my intentions and fears, my every thought in that single gaze.

"Curious creature." Her words slowly slurred across her tongue in a raspy voice. I took a step back in panic and Beck's nose brushed fearfully against the side of my leg.

"Your stumbling by was no accident or coincidence. You were meant to come at this time," the old woman said.

I instantly felt regret for having stumbled here. It was obvious she wasn't all mentally there, and I wished I could just walk away and leave her to herself.

I let out a quick, uneasy laugh as I exhaled. "I, I think you have me mixed up with someone else. We were just passing by—"

"You came to this life, at this time, with a purpose," she interrupted. "I can see it. You are a balancer." Her old, shriveled finger trembled as she reached and pointed it towards me.

My muscles began to tense up, pulling my shoulder blades in closer to my backbone. Despite sounding insane, there was something captivating about her character that invited me in and I felt a strange desire to believe her words.

"What do you mean *balancer*?" My feet began to slowly step forward as I hungered to learn more.

Each word was drawn out and diluted by her struggling breaths as she spoke. "I see it in your aura. So curious. You are much different from the others."

Her words were like a familiar riddle with the answer just beyond my reach. The truth vacuumed into darkness and all my senses leapt to escape the silence, yearning to discover the knowledge she held.

"I don't understand," I said.

She reached for the rickety sideboards of the doorway and struggled as she pulled herself up. She was small, but the measure of her physical size did little to muffle the inexplicable intimidation of her presence. Her old-fashioned dress hung low as a lifeless shade of deep grey. She looked as though she could have been a century old with her rounded shoulders hunched forward causing her spine to bulge out and display the bone joints trailing down her backside.

"Would you like me to show you . . . what I can see?" she asked.

She reached out with her palm extended toward me, inviting me closer. I stood still, trying to render my sense of judgment. I was afraid, but my curiosity grew and began to overrule my fear.

I felt my feet hesitantly drag themselves in her direction until we stood face to face. She raised both of her frail hands in front of me and whispered, "Close your eyes."

Terrified, I did as instructed and felt her cold, wrinkled fingers lightly touch the soft skin of my eyelids.

Warps of churning colors floating in every direction suddenly overtook my vision. It felt as though my entire body was soaring backwards in a high-speed jet plane. The colors traveled around me like people, bumping against each other and wandering in their own, separate spaces.

I heard shadows of jabbering and laughter reverberate in every direction. Some were loud while others moved quietly from place to place. I suddenly realized these moving shapes were humans. It became clear how this woman was able to see me without the sense of sight. This must be how she discerned the people around her.

The hallucination changed and I watched from a distance as these energies of color moved to sit in small groups, clustered around what must be tables and benches.

I recognized Shyler's voice above all the chattering. "So, this scholarship program I was telling you about earlier, for the Kenneth Adams Foundation. I should have my application complete by the end of this week. Did you get a chance to look at the link I sent you?"

This was a memory. I was seeing the cafeteria from earlier this afternoon through new eyes. Almost like my life was overlapping a world of different visual perception.

I scanned through all the waves of energy and compared the variation of brightness and radiation in each individual. My eyes focused on a peculiar shape whose color was unique from the others but who struggled to shine. The swirling spirit seemed dim and faded, hidden deep inside of its body structure. I then recognized that the personage I was studying was myself.

I was completely different from the others. It was evidence of the unclear feelings I had always felt deep inside. My aura was undeniably mismatched from everyone else around me.

I watched the form of the skinny girl in the distance humiliated again by the vivid shapes of the terrorizing boys kicking her lunch. As I saw the act repeated, I remembered my defensive anger desiring to make the bullying stop.

The contrasting color inside my peculiar frame suddenly began to boil. It throbbed powerfully and grew brighter and stronger. The energy was brilliant and clear, yet it trembled in my form, fighting to escape.

I felt the hands of the blind witch release, and the vision dissolved from my view. Stumbling backward, I quickly tried regaining my balance. I leaned forward and grabbed my knees to concentrate on controlling the spinning vertigo slamming against my head.

"What was that energy inside of me? Why was I so different from everyone else?" I struggled to puzzle together this freshly taken-in vision as it wrestled to disintegrate from my memory.

"Every soul on this Earth has been born with a specific purpose. We have all been given gifts. Some are fortunate enough to discover the powers in themselves and find access to these abilities," she said.

I turned over my hand and studied the soft skin of my palm as my thumb kneaded over its surface. My eyes tried pushing past my plain sight, desperate to again see the illuminating colors flowing through me.

"Most are common gifts: understanding, courage, compassion. But you are most certainly uncommon, balancer."

"What does it mean?" I asked.

The woman tilted her head up toward the clouded sky. She closed her eyes as if to soak up imaginary rain dropping onto her leathery skin.

"You are a vessel with a great power that continuously flows within you. Unlock that power and you become a doorway," she explained.

"A doorway to what? Why can't I access it?" I asked. "I saw that energy trapped inside of me, wanting to break out."

I began to feel frustrated. My whole life's purpose seemed hidden from my understanding, and now, as I was handed an instrument to find this purpose, I had no idea how it could be controlled. I couldn't let this chance go to discover who I really was.

The hermit woman shuffled back and reached inside the doorway. I listened as the wood of the floorboards groaned under her bandaged feet. She dragged out a dirty, worn basket full of hand-carved lava rocks. The twined material was covered in dust and mended with tiny white webs.

Her yellow fingernails rummaged through the pile and stopped to pick out a black stone that glimmered like glass. Her other hand reached into her pocket and pulled out a small, steel knife.

I backed up immediately, and Beck began to growl again. The witch-like woman disregarded our startled reactions and continued with her task.

"To release the flame, one needs to first ignite the spark," she explained. She quickly scraped the rock and knife together, making a glint of fire bounce and land on a small pile of weeds. She crouched down low and blew on the sparks, causing a simmering glow to pulse through the birthing smoke.

"A common gift can be unlocked as easily as being aware of one's self. A journey of self-discovery, you could say."

Her weak body traveled around the cobwebbed shack as she searched through her piles of strange trinkets and collections. Underneath a faded cloth, she gently pulled out a dark object in the shape of a well-crafted hand mirror. Her hands stroked the edges to wipe away the dust and smudges.

"But I can see with a unique gift like yours, a little extra help may be necessary," she explained.

I glanced again at the mirror in her hand. The smooth, black material of the reflector seemed to be made of a polished stone with little speckles of glowing silver that stood out in the angle of light.

"Onyx," she explained as she sensed my curiosity. "If

one pays close attention, it can reveal worlds of mystery: secrets, the passage of time, and of course, unlocking our inner energies."

I stepped backwards as she hobbled outside and made her way toward a nearby tree stump. She placed the mirror face down and continued to trace its back outline with her mud-stained fingers before turning back. She seemed to have a deep love and connection to the black reflection, almost as if her soul was enslaved to it.

I was completely mesmerized by the mirror as well. The strength of self-control had to hold me back as my feet desperately longed to gravitate toward it.

"So, what? All I need to do is look at myself in the mirror to *spark* this power inside me?" I asked looking back at the small pile of smoking weeds.

"Take caution when making this choice. This is not a decision to take lightly, young one." Her tone was deeper and more serious than ever. "You must choose to keep what's inside of you locked away and leave now, living your life the way you always have, or to unleash it. But once it is let loose, you can never summon back what has been undone. Your life and your path *will* be changed forever."

The white eyes of the woman gazed down at the mirror as she breathed in deeply through her open jaw. Her tongue traced the borders of her mouth and wet her crinkled lips.

"You will become connected to those who have gazed in the mirror before you. Be cautious of this very serious reality. They can be . . . unpredictable."

She released her fingers from the mirror and turned to leave, limping into the thick wilderness.

"They?" I mumbled under my breath.

I stared at the tree trunk as my fumbling fingers tottered at my sides. I sensed the high risk of danger lingering in the consequences of looking in the mirror.

"Will bad things happen if I choose this?" I asked.

The hermit paused and turned back toward me. The silence of the surrounding woods poured through me like cold water as I waited for her response.

"If a fish were given the gift to grow wings, would it choose to be free and discover the mountains and mystical lands only heard of in stories? Or would it reject the gift and stay safe in its pond, away from the dangers outside the world it has always known?"

She turned back and continued on her way. One could sense the ache in her joints with each delicate step she took. Inside me, there was one last question desperate to escape my lack of understanding.

"Your eyes . . . How did it happen?"

She stopped in her footsteps and stood still without turning. I could feel that my words upset her and the fear of danger she caused to rattle inside me unleashed again. Down at my side, Beck turned on her defensive mode and began barking once more.

"Beck, hush!" I said as I reached down and rubbed her fur to sooth her. I looked back up to find that the woman had vanished. The trees stood empty and alone with no sign of her in any direction.

A sharp chill ran down my spine. The chill was so strong, it felt as though icy fingers had touched the back of my neck and slowly slid down my skin. I pulled up the collar of my jacket and covered my ears in an attempt to stop my body from shivering.

I eyed the black mirror still sitting on the stump. *My life will never be the same,* I told myself as the mirror tempted me in its direction. *What if it's dangerous? How can I trust this witch woman? What if it's all a trick?*

Turn away. Go home! My mind screamed at me in

warning. *Run back to the world you know.* It was too risky. It was foolish enough that I had already stayed this long.

"C'mon, Beck," I said and quickly turned to head back in the direction of the house. I resisted the powerful temptation of the mirror and we began walking home.

Suddenly, I heard Shyler's voice echoing in my mind, and I remembered the question she had asked me earlier that day, "Don't you ever feel like you were meant for bigger things?"

My shoes planted in the soil beneath me, and I felt the weight of regret rooting my feet into the ground. I looked back up the hill towards the isolated hut.

I felt a sudden, unexplainable glimmer of hope and warmth radiate inside me. Perhaps it was my locked energy and power desiring to burst out. Whatever was happening, the emotion was so strong that my body began trembling. Beck sensed my distress and began to whimper.

I shot around and ran towards the shack, back to the lonely tree stump. My legs flew beneath me in quick rhythm as my focus zoned in on my one goal. I reached out snatching the mirror in my hands. When I held it upside-down, I paused before finally turning over the surface that revealed my reflection.

I had prepared myself for a mystical image of wondering awe in the stone's smooth frame but was disappointed to see nothing but my plain, colorless face staring back through the black onyx.

Etched in the dark handle was an unfamiliar symbol. Curved lines stretched out and swept along its surface, like the tangled branches of a giant tree. Scattered shapes buried themselves into the image like dangling fruits holding to their rooted lifeline inside the tree limbs.

I tipped my wrist to the side to observe the silver streaks emit the sunlight and watched my face stretch out from the middle of the reflection to the rounded corners.

As I tilted the angle back to the center, I saw in the scenery's gap of bright sky the reflection of a menacing man peering out from behind my shoulder.

His frightening face made me scream out and drop the mirror, shattering it into hundreds of tiny fragments. They scattered in the mix of pine needles blanketing the roots of the large tree trunk.

I turned toward a sound of rustling bushes behind me, and Beck again began to bark aggressively. Frantically, I stepped back as a sharp movement in the tall, dry grass made its way toward me. I had lost the ability to breathe and trembled as it rapidly approached.

Suddenly, at the bottom of the pathway of bushes, a large raccoon waddled out into the clearing.

Beck leaped toward the whiskered intruder and chased it as it scampered quickly into a nearby tree, hissing back at us from the tall branches.

I dropped to my knees, relieved and worn out from the unnecessary anxiety. I fingered through the pieces of shattered mirror spread out across the soil and placed a few large, sharp fragments in a pile on top of the trunk.

"Beck, we have to go now," I called.

I quickly stumbled back down the hillside for home. This was definitely enough adventure for one day.

I reviewed the words of the hermit and wondered what could have gone wrong. *Why didn't the mirror change me?* I was full of disappointment as I concluded that I would most likely never see the strange woman again. And especially that I was nothing out of the ordinary and that my world would never change.

Chapter 3

Voicemail from Mom, received 6 PM today:

"Rylee, will you pick up some milk at the market on your way home? I totally spaced it when I was out today! Your mom is losing her mind. Thanks, Honey. Love you."

I had gone straight to Shyler's house after school to drop off one of her fall sweaters I had recently borrowed. Shyler was my apparel library where I made frequent exchanges of her rarely used outfits. She went on countless Portland shopping trips with her mother across the river, making it impossible to find an article of clothing in her closet that wasn't fabulous.

Mom's last minute request synced perfectly with the timing of my drive home. After listening to her message, I changed directions and steered into the grocery parking lot. In the passenger's seat of the car my cell phone began beeping, warning me of its low battery. I sighed in relief, thankful that I was able to catch the voicemail before the phone died.

Trying to avoid as many friendly neighbors as I possibly could to keep from getting trapped in a never-ending conversation, I walked briskly to the back of the store with my head low and grabbed two gallons of milk.

Voices traveled over the low aisles and I listened to a couple humorously argue back and forth.

"Orange!? Where'd you get the bright idea to pick out an orange sweater, Jerry?! You want me to walk around town looking like a Halloween pumpkin?!"

Curiosity got the better of me as I peaked around the corner and watched a short, pregnant woman nagging her husband.

When I approached the front of the line to pay, the cashier hardly acknowledged my presence as she stood and vented to the grocery bagger about her boyfriend forgetting to pick up her son after school.

She held out my change without looking in my direction. I gently pulled it from her periwinkle fingernails and sarcastically thanked her for her help. Before I finished walking out the sliding glass door, I could hear the pregnant woman complaining to the cashier as she unloaded her shopping cart. It was secretly fulfilling watching the unpleasant cashier greeted with more unpleasantness.

By the time I made it back out to the car it was nearly dark. I only drove a few miles out of the busier part of town and found myself on a quiet road with no other vehicles in sight.

Alone with my thoughts, I began to brainstorm what jeans would look best with the boots I had borrowed from Shyler when the car made a sudden, loud thud and jerked aggressively to the side. I gasped, tightly gripping the wheel and slammed both of my feet on the brake pedal to steady the wild commotion.

I must have a flat. Dang it. Trying not to panic, I switched on my hazard lights and pulled off to the shoulder of the road. I looked down at the empty screen of my cell phone.

"Dead battery," I laughed. "Wonderful."

As I swung the car door open, the only sound I heard was the single-toned beeping of the seatbelt alarm. Outside everything was chillingly quiet. I took a deep breath to calm my nerves and reached into the glove box, pulling out a heavy flashlight.

The journey from the front door around to the back of the car felt almost unreachable in the darkness. I stared straight down at my shuffling shoes to distract my wandering thoughts. Ever since peering into the stone mirror, my imagination would cloud with the frightening face of the strange man whenever I found myself alone. I shook my head to rattle away the unpleasant nightmare.

After verifying which car wheel was punctured, I popped open the trunk hoping my dad's mundane lessons of changing a tire would refresh in my mind by the time I pulled out the necessary tools.

"Let's see, I need a wrench and Dad always mentioned something about a lug nut. What's a lug nut again? Where's that jack?" As I fumbled through the back, I watched my shadow expand in front of me, exposed in a sudden bright beam of light. I turned around to see the headlights of an old pickup truck pulling over. My hand covered my squinting eyes to block the blinding brightness.

"Looks like you could use a hand!" The shout came from an older voice with a slight country accent. An old, thin man hopped out wearing farmer jeans, worn out tennis shoes, and a plaid, long-sleeved shirt. In the faint darkness beside the truck, I could see his white hair barely stick out from beneath his baseball cap.

Dale was one of our close neighbors and had been a family friend for as long as I could remember. Before retiring, he had worked for the cherry orchards, helping out during the season for fifty years. After that, he spent almost every day taking his boat out fishing on the Columbia catching squawfish.

The state paid a small bounty on squaws to keep them from eating the salmon eggs in the river. "It pays for ma' boat gas," he would say every time he went out to fish.

He was a kind man, always going out of his way to help those around him. Life was his blessed opportunity to serve as many of his fellowmen as possible. I don't think I ever saw him do anything without a sincere smile.

"Hey, Dale. I think I've got a flat," I said, relieved to see a familiar face.

He insisted on managing everything himself, so I stood back gratefully and watched. His wrinkled fingers worked carefully as he cranked the jack and positioned the spare tire into place. I was so relieved that he had stopped for me. There was no way I would have remembered all of the steps to change it on my own.

"Thank you, Dale. You're a life saver."

"Just glad I could help, Rylee. You take care now, ya hear?" He opened my driver's door like a gentleman and patted the top of the car before walking away. I stalled and waited for him to get safely back to his truck before starting the engine. Dale pulled off his hat and waved out the window as he pulled back onto the road.

While I watched his truck disappear in the distance, I was overwhelmed by the amount of kindness in one man. I smiled thinking about how much Dale deserved for everything he always did to help out around the town. It wasn't so much a prayer but a moment of urgent reflection as I wished for him to be truly happy.

I sat and concentrated on this sincere desire and immediately felt a strange unlocking in my soul. It was a literal sensation escaping me that I had never experienced before, like water pouring out of a bucket inside my heart.

Whatever it was, it pulled itself outside of me and floated away in Dale's direction.

Wednesday morning Dad sat in his recliner checking his e-mails and notifications on his tablet. He leaned back and propped up his worn-out slippers, adjusted his reading glasses, and took a sip of his daily spinach breakfast smoothie. He yawned and scratched at the stubble of whiskers growing underneath his chin. Bags of dark circles underlined his puffy eyes, and his morning hair shot out in every direction.

"Rylee, I'm taking you to school today. I'll drop your car off at the shop this afternoon to have them switch all the tires. Can you get a ride home?" he asked.

Lame. I loved having the independence of driving. It was the one freedom I had a hard time functioning without.

I sighed.

"Could I drive it to school and then you or Mom pick it up in the parking lot on your way to the shop? It's just down the street?"

Dad eyed me, slightly irritated.

"Aaaaaand I'll sweep the back porch for you," I added.

"Deal," he mumbled and continued with his morning reading. He seemed deeply interested in a local article he had pulled up from the daily news.

"Ha! Will you look at that? Dale from down the street finally won that treasure home raffle this morning," he chuckled.

I froze at the kitchen counter with my plate piled high with scrambled eggs and flat cakes.

"He did what?" I asked. I looked down and had to stop myself from coating my entire breakfast with maple syrup.

"It's the same one he enters every year for charity.

He can pick the cash prize or that giant mansion they're giving away down in San Diego. I don't believe it." Dad shook his head and continued reading.

Lucky Dale.

How funny that I just saw him last night, and today something like this happens. I thought back to his kind service of going out of his way to change my flat. This lottery was perfect for him. I smiled, thinking about how all of his kindness over the years had finally paid off. A better person could not have won.

Everything feels balanced, I thought. Even as I said the words in my mind, I began to piece together segments of recent memories: the balancer, the mirror, the hermit witch. *Is it a coincidence? Do I have something to do with this?*

My fork slipped out of my hand and dropped on the kitchen floor. It bounced across the tile and smacked Beck right in the face who was waiting patiently for scraps to fall out of Harrison's breakfast bowl. Startled by the fork, she bolted out from underneath the table knocking over a chair as her nails clicked like a melody across the floor. Over and over again, her furry paws skidded underneath her, giving the action a cartoonish look of running in place.

"Sorry, Beck!" I yelled as she yelped and hid in the other room. Harrison flung his head back and roared with laughter. Dad glanced over for a brief second then continued with his reading.

Distracted by the serendipitous occurrence with Dale, I was no longer hungry. Trying to seem casual, I took my plate to the sink.

Without thought or reason, Harrison flung a cereal oat in my direction that splashed right between my eyes.

"Really, child?" I asked, dismissively. My brother had

a special place in my heart, and no matter how much of a pest he was, my filter of patience rarely ran out. I was always very protective of Harrison and had the inability to stay upset with him in his innocent stage of childhood.

He giggled with a mouth full of cereal as milk ran down his chin. Shifting his body as I walked away from the sink, he accidentally swept his entire bowl of soggy oaks into his lap.

"C'mon, Harris! You're making a huge mess!" Dad exclaimed across the room. Beck sneaked back into the kitchen and began lapping up the puddle of milk as it ran between the cracks of the tiles. I ruffled my brother's hair and left him soaking in his sticky chair as I made my way back upstairs to change.

On my drive to school, I adjusted the rearview mirror and caught a glimpse of the rounded sunglasses hiding my eyes. A smile crept across my face as I soaked in the thrill of gliding around the curved corners of the pavement. I gripped the steering wheel tight, still a little anxious from my prior experience with the popped tire, but not enough to stop loving the rush I felt from controlling the movement of the car.

I pulled up to a crosswalk and waited for a jogger to pass by before turning. The truck following behind me, not realizing I had to yield, let out an impatient honk. I looked back to see a younger man badly in need of a haircut throw his hands in the air in a fit of road rage.

"Oh no, he'll arrive at work a whole ten seconds later than originally planned," I said to myself and laughed. To further my amusement, I took my sweet time and waited an additional few seconds before finally making my turn.

I heard him peel out behind me and glanced in my mirror in time to catch a long finger sticking up out of the roof as he yelled in my direction.

"You are a sweetheart," I mumbled under my breath. There was suddenly a slight tingling inside me. It was the same detachment I had felt escape through my soul as Dale had driven away the night before. This time it gravitated in the direction of the livid driver. The feeling was dim and clouded, much different than my previous experience.

Not a second later, I looked back again and saw flashes of bright blue and red lights flying by. I listened to the sound of a police siren follow the route of the angry truck driver.

"Yes!" I laughed as I watched the officer pull the vehicle over. "Sweet justice!" My hands covered my mouth in shock as I reviewed the bad luck just witnessed. I thought of Dale and the lottery. Then Harris throwing his cereal at me while the rest spilled into his lap. Everything perfectly pieced together like molding shapes of clay. I couldn't believe it.

Ever since that day I had stumbled upon the old shack and the hermit everything was different. Everyone I interacted with somehow received immediate justice for the way they treated me. A chill shot up my spine. *This is real. This is really happening to me. This is the power that was locked inside of me.*

I pulled into the school parking lot, shut off the engine, and waited inside the car.

"I have to practice on someone," I whispered. There was still a portion of me that refused to believe this shocking reality, and I had to prove it to myself.

I scanned the parking lot, seeking my own personal lab rat. Examining the faces of every student, I searched for someone predictable I could attempt to alter.

Suddenly I saw the thin, quiet girl from the cafeteria walk past my car and into the building. Ideas churned together in my brain as I strived to develop a plan.

When lunch came around, I spotted her in the crowd. I grabbed an apple and small soda bottle, placing them neatly on a plastic lunch tray. As she made her way to her normal spot alone on the floor, I smiled and approached her.

"May I sit next to you today?" I asked politely. I felt slightly guilty about my request. Seeing her sit alone every day, I had never offered a kind gesture of friendship before now.

Puzzled, she nodded and moved her backpack to clear a spot beside her. As I set the tray down near my feet, she flashed a shy smile and pulled her hair back behind her ears. I bit my lip and looked down, thinking of what I could say to liven the conversation.

"Cool shoes." Nice. I'm so awkward at times.

She pulled up her legs and examined her neon green tennies from a sideways angle. She smiled again and turned to eat her lunch.

As we chewed in silence, an echo of laughter traveled in our direction from down the hallway. Beside me, the girl shrank down, tugging on her sweatshirt to cover the sides of her face. Without even looking up, she knew that the gang of bullies was making its daily journey to the lunchroom. I watched as she awaited the traditional agonizing encounter.

The leader eyed his prey as he turned the corner and cracked his spiked knuckles. I peered over my new lunch mate's shoulder to get a better look as the group made their way toward us. With the tip of my foot, I slightly pushed my lunch tray out into the open, giving the cruel boys an open invitation for their predictable destruction.

The leader's eyes lit up as he spotted the perfectly placed soda bottle. I secretly held a comparable level of excitement, hoping for this chance to again test out my newly discovered gift. If his actions were intended to affect me in an unkind way, perhaps his negative consequences would unravel before our very eyes. We could watch the balance of natural justice slap him right back in his unpleasant face.

He skipped up to the tray and quickly snatched the bottled drink.

"I'll take this," he sang and flipped it in his hand. His trail of minions chuckled closely behind him.

After a few more steps, he tossed it in the air and drew back his foot. As the soda began to fall to the ground he quickly kicked forward, punting it across the cafeteria.

The lid of the bottle popped off right as it connected with his foot and sticky liquid sprayed over his entire body. His jeans, T-shirt, and jacket were covered in dripping, brown liquid.

As the crowded cafeteria howled with laughter, the empty bottle rolled across the floor and stopped directly in front of the leather shoes of Principal O'Connors. He eyed the young man with a cold expression.

Without a word, he pointed down the hallway and followed as the bully waddled in his soiled clothes to the principal's office. The lunchroom went wild with delight while they watched their classmate trudge the walk of shame.

The thin girl giggled seeing her tormenter leave in humility. I leaned back against the wall and smiled. *I found it,* I thought to myself. *I've discovered my gift and who I'm supposed to be. I am the balancer.*

Chapter 4

I rushed through the gym doors and made a beeline for Shyler. She was holding a huge plate of french fries bathed in melted cheese and fry sauce. I grabbed her arm and without a word pulled her in the direction of the bleachers.

"Well, hello. It's nice to see you too. French fry?"

I dragged her to a side section of benches where we could talk alone. Besides a couple of staggered students studying and a group of boys scrimmaging a game of basketball, there were no other people nearby.

"Are you okay?" She could tell I had something on my mind by the lack of friendly conversation.

"I need you to test something for me," I replied. Removing all possible distractions, I gently pulled the tray of fries from her hands and set them on the floor by her feet.

"Okay," Shyler responded, curious. She tucked one of her long legs underneath her, trying to adjust to the uncomfortable bleachers.

I took in a deep breath. *She's going to think I'm crazy.*

"I really need you to be open-minded."

She opened both of her hands in front of her, with her palms facing out toward me.

"My mind is open."

Her fingers fluttered and closed into a fist as she placed her hands back down in her lap. She was always very dramatic and enjoyed the theatrics of body language.

"Okay." I nervously attempted to put my thoughts into words. The sound of squeaking sneakers on the basketball court aggravated my concentration like constant dripping water in a broken sink.

"Think of all those sci-fi and fairy-tale magic movies you always made me watch with you when we were kids, about time travel, and mutant powers, and . . . and . . . bright polka-dot unicorns. *That* kind of open mind."

She looked at me cautiously.

"Are you hiding a unicorn in your backyard? Because I KNEW there was a reason your dad always kept the door locked on that brick shed!"

"Shyler, what? No! Listen," I paused for a second and watched her wait patiently for me to reveal the inconceivable skeleton that was painfully shoved in my closet of hidden secrets. I pulled an elastic tie from my pocket and began pulling my hair back into a thick, messy bun.

"I need you to slap me," I told her.

"Slap you? Ha! No! You are so odd," she responded and looked over her shoulder to see if anyone nearby could pick up on our conversation.

"Just do it!"

"I'm not going to!"

"Trust me!"

"No, Rylee. Stop it."

We bickered back and forth until finally she stretched back her hand and whacked the back of my skull, making a loud slap sound echo through the gym. At that precise moment, the basketball from the boys' game down below went flying through the air and smacked hard on the back of Shyler's head.

"Ouch! Holy crap!"

She massaged her fingers through the back of her short hair as the rubber ball bounced back down the bleachers.

"Sorry," one of the players called out as he raised his hand apologetically.

Shyler's face went red as she turned back toward me, covering her profile with an open hand to shield her embarrassment.

"So, what exactly was the point of me slapping you?"

"The basketball . . . THAT happened because of what you just did to me!" I said.

She scowled at me with a jumbled look of puzzlement.

"What are you talking about?" She reached up to the back of her head to rub the throbbing pain that still lingered.

"Whenever people are unkind to me, bad things happen to them. And when they do something positive, all of the sudden they get good luck! I'm like . . . the gate-keeper of retribution or something. I don't know what's going on!"

She looked confused and skeptical. Her eyebrows dropped, and her lips pouted as if she had tasted something sour and unpleasant, but in her eyes I could tell she was trying to believe me.

"So, I hurt you, and I get hurt?" she asked, rearranging the logic revolving through her thoughts.

"Yes." I nodded my head.

"And if I do something nice, something great will supposedly happen to me?"

"I think so," I replied.

Shyler twisted in her seat and searched around her. She reached for her still untouched plate of french fries and started to hand them to me. There was a half a second of hesitation.

"This is a BIG deal and a genuine sacrifice for me. I REALLY wanted to eat these," she said, handing me her plate. "Take them. Eat every last delicious bite for me. I am an amazing friend trying to show an act of kindness right now." I grinned at her testing strategy.

"I do know how much these mean to you. You love food."

"Yes. Yes I do. More than most of my living family members."

I held them in my lap and we sat quietly. We waited. Nothing happened. Shyler's shoe began to tap impatiently.

I interrupted the silence. "Well, sometimes I have to concentrate to get it to work. Maybe I have to master this before it comes automatically."

She sighed and tried looking away to distract herself from the passing time.

I selected a fry and began to examine it. I watched the dripping, melted cheese and smiled thinking of Shyler's little sacrifice. As I thought about our warm years of friendship it felt as though a thin layer of skin began to peel off of my heart and evaporate into that familiar energy. Something was working.

In the background we heard a timid woman's voice over the intercom, "Shyler Clarke, please report to the principal's office. Shyler Clarke to the principal. Thank you." Click.

Her eyes opened wide. Laughter grew on the basketball court as the boys began teasing Shyler when they heard her name announced.

"Now I'm in trouble apparently. I thought you said kindness brought *good* luck," she whispered to me as she stood up. I followed her out of the gym and walked her through the school to the main office.

As we approached the secretary's desk, I noticed the bully in the corner, still soaked in soda. His lower lip pouted into a solid frown as he tried to continue faking his tough character to cover the embarrassment haunting him from earlier. I snickered under my breath as his moist shoes squished underneath his knees nervously bouncing in place.

Principal O'Connors was waiting calmly behind his desk as we both walked inside. In the corner of the room, a small woman in a buttoned up, maroon dress sat with a notebook and a pile of folders in her lap.

"Hello, ladies. Shyler, I wanted to introduce you to Miss Smith. She's here representing the Kenneth Adams Foundation and earlier she reviewed your application for their scholarship program."

Shyler turned and stared at me in disbelief.

"Hello, Shyler, it's a pleasure to meet you." The woman stood up and reached out to shake her hand. Knowing how much this meant to her, I watched Shyler glow with excitement as her hand met Miss Smith's.

I quietly stepped back out of the office and shut the door behind me. Smiling, I reached down and took a bite of tasty cheese fries.

To kill time while Shyler met with the principal and Miss Smith, I walked across the hallway to the library. Kids sat silently wearing headphones, typing on desktop computers, and hunting through piles of textbooks.

I casually scanned the dusty shelves and came across a thick book about identifying rocks and flipped to find information on the onyx mineral to keep myself entertained. Over in the corner, I found a big empty love sack to settle in and made myself comfortable.

A female student was walking around the room with

a camera strapped around her shoulder. She searched the library for any students willing to smile for her pictures. Some would comically pose as if they were passionately reading, lost in their schoolwork, while others crowded close together and flashed their perfect grins on the count of three.

Uneasy about the attention that accompanied cameras, I was determined not to participate in the picture taking. I fumbled through my bag and pulled out a pair of light prescription glasses. I shielded them over my eyes to hide behind and pulled my book up close to my face to appear deep in study, hoping to give off the vibe that I wasn't in the mood to be disturbed.

"You seem intensely occupied in your reading," a familiar, deep voice said in front of me. I tilted down my book to see Merritt's charming smile.

"Room for two?" he asked and nudged his way onto the love sack. Without his hat on, he looked more like the Merritt I remembered from when we were younger. His wavy, brown curls seemed to have tamed down since childhood, but each strand still had its defining spiral shape.

I laughed. "I'm in stealth mode, attempting to avoid camera lady."

She turned her head and caught the two of us in the corner of her eye. A smirk stretched across her face, and she began making her way toward us from the other side of the room.

"Well, I thought you were doing a great job. You totally have the intimidating librarian look down," he said.

"I look like a librarian lady?" I whispered as the photographer came closer. *Is that some kind of insult?* I thought to myself.

He pointed to my face.

"I mean, you're totally rocking the nerdy glasses and bun. You look great!" he laughed. I had forgotten about my hair I had pulled back earlier in the gym before asking Shyler to hit me.

The lady with the camera interrupted our conversation, "May I get a photo of you two for the yearbook?"

I sighed. There was no way of getting out of a picture now.

I also wanted to show Merritt how "un-librarian" I was capable of looking. In one fluid motion, I stripped off my glasses and tugged out my bun. I ran my fingers through my hair, smoothing its billows as it dropped gracefully to the sides.

"We'd love to," I said without breaking eye contact with Merritt. My transition from librarian geek to a girl of confidence must have amused him as he stared back at me with a half smile, studying my face.

"Well, you guys have to actually look at the camera," she said a little annoyed, trying to win back our attention. Our eyes remained locked for an extra second before we turned to the camera lens.

"Smile!" she sang. The quick flash stung the sockets of my eyes. As I blinked rapidly, little squares of negative black flashes continuously slid down my line of vision.

She looked down at her camera and waited for the picture to appear on her display screen. After a moment she nodded, satisfied with our smiles, and walked away without another word.

I turned back to Merritt who was surveying me in deep thought. His hand was touching his face as his knuckles subtly brushed his bottom lip.

"What?" I asked, trying to read his thoughts. Up close I could see that his childhood freckles also seemed to have faded over the years. They had mostly disappeared besides an exceptional few that sprinkled across his nose and under his eyes.

Enthusiastically he replied, "Honestly, I think the librarian look was ridiculously attractive."

I laughed and tried pushing him away. Resisting, he pulled himself in closer and turned toward me so his chest pressed against my shoulder.

"Do you own, like, fifty cats?" he whispered.

"Oh my gosh, you need to stop talking."

"Does the ankle length night gown you wear to bed match your purple, granny slippers? I knew it!" he chuckled.

"Rylee, there you are!" I looked over to see Shyler entering the library across the room. She sped over to me and grabbed my arm.

"We really need to talk about what just happened with Mr. O'Connors." She pulled me out of the seat with urgency and glanced over at Merritt. "Hello, Merritt. You're looking gorgeous as always. So sorry to break you two up, but this is kind of an emergency." My cheeks began to blush as she ripped me away and started pulling me out the door.

I looked over my shoulder at him and smiled. "Um, I'll see you around, I guess." He nodded his head and grinned back.

As we left the room, I tried to shake his captivating smile from my mind so I could focus on Shyler. The distraction of Merritt made me momentarily forget about my exciting, newly discovered ability. Things in my life were definitely in the process of dramatic changes.

Chapter 5

Scratch. Scratch. Scratch. My zigzag doodles in the top corner of my homework somehow morphed into actual slits shredding through the page with the sharp edge of my pencil lead.

"Anything on your mind, honey?" I had almost forgotten that my mom was standing there washing dishes in the kitchen. The unexpected sound of her voice made me jump.

"No, I'm just . . . thinking. Not a big fan of statistics I guess," I replied. I was so distracted by today's unexplainable events that concentrating on my studies seemed entirely impossible. Excitement began to wear off and transitioned to deep worry of the unknown. I started thinking about my future, how my whole world would now be different.

What if this is too much for me to handle? What if I make a mistake? What if I am a mistake?

Mom turned off the water and started drying her hands. Her crossing from the sink to the kitchen table seemed to take a lot more energy than normal. She grabbed the back of the wooden chair for support, and her skinny arms almost trembled as she lowered herself into the seat across from mine.

"Are you feeling all right, Mom?" I asked as I watched her sit in exhaustion.

"I'm just drained. Worked too hard in the yard today. But I'll get a good night sleep, so I can't complain."

I had never heard her complain. Of all the people I had encountered throughout my life, she was probably the most positive person I knew. Even more than Dale.

Once when I was little, we ordered a giant pizza for dinner. As I set the table, I lifted the delivery box to tuck the cardboard lid underneath for extra room. I was so focused on positioning the lid that without realizing it, I tilted the top just enough for the entire pizza to slide out of my hands and fall flat on the carpet. The room fell silent. I closed my eyes and braced myself for a severe tongue-lashing, but instead I heard my mother's faint giggle.

"Okay," she laughed. "Change of dinner plans. Everyone to the car!" She squeezed my shoulder and kissed the top of my head. Her legs crouched down so she was kneeling eye level in front of me.

"I dropped Grandma's lemon meringue pie all over the kitchen floor once when I was your age," she whispered to me. "You should have seen the look on her face! But guess what? We just cleaned it up and made another pie that was even prettier and more delicious that the first one." I could always count on her to see the good in everything.

"So, maybe it's not my math homework that's bugging me," I admitted.

"What's wrong?" She waited for my answer with deep concern as if she could sense the amount of stress pressing down on me.

I didn't want to tell her anything about the mirror or the witch in the woods. She would freak out knowing I was mingling with strangers in the middle of the wilderness. I feared my story would concern my family, making them believe I had gone insane and be sent to some kind of mental institution. Besides telling Shyler about my new gift, everything else had to remain my secret and mine alone.

"Things have just been weird lately. I feel like . . . like . . . Do you ever feel like you were . . . a mistake? Not a *mistake*! Just like something's not right and maybe things got mixed up and you weren't meant to be the way you are? Like life made a mistake?"

I was always capable of making a simple thought sound as complex and confusing as humanly possible. Communication was hardly one of my strengths.

There was no judgmental look in her face. In her eyes, all I could see was sincerity. She was great like that. I could tell her anything and know she was genuinely listening to me. My mother would mentally step outside of her perspective and view any situation wholly from the other person's shoes.

She took a deep breath before answering.

"Your father and I were married for eight years before you were born. We tried everything to start a family, but there isn't much a woman can do to get pregnant with lifeless ovaries." She giggled again to herself with a slight hint of pain, reflecting on the past.

Looking down, she examining her hands while she talked. She had beautiful hands. I always thought her thin, long fingers would have been perfect for playing the piano, stretching out gracefully across the keys. They were still slightly wet from the dishwater.

"For months and months I would cry myself to sleep." She paused.

Eight years? I had no idea it had taken them that long. I guess the timeline had always been accessible for me to calculate, but it was never something that had crossed my mind. I noticed her eyes begin to sparkle as they filled with water.

"I missed you before you were born, Rylee. There was a hole in my heart that couldn't be filled." Two small tears ran down each side of her face, almost in unison. Somehow my mom managed to still look graceful as she cried.

"I knew I would be a mother. And once I realized the timing just wasn't right, I knew you would come when you were supposed to come. I knew there was a reason for everything, a perfect timetable beyond my understanding, and that you were a pretty special soul who was meant to come into our lives at the exact time that you came."

I reached out and touched her beautiful hands. She was so in tune with what people needed to hear at the exact time they needed to hear it.

"You were SUPPOSED to come here, Rylee."

The hallow cavities in my chest absorbed her warm words. In the back of my mind I could see the hermit and remembered her similar words. I was meant to come to this life, at this time, with a purpose.

Mom got up and began cleaning dishes again.

You were supposed to come here, I told myself. I quickly snatched my textbook and papers to head upstairs for the night.

Ouch! I looked down at my ripped-up paper corner next to my finger that began bleeding. Paper cut. *Just my luck.*

Chapter 6

I don't know how I got persuaded into taking Religions of the World as one of my elective classes. Mr. Craven's classroom was always far too hot, making it nearly impossible to stay awake.

I leaned backwards and stretched out my ribcage, hoping more oxygen to the brain would help increase my alertness. I glanced over at my classmates who all seemed to share the same lack of enthusiasm.

Addison sat cross-legged inspecting the tips of her hair, searching for hidden split ends. She always puffed out her luscious lips, reminding me of my dad's food allergy reaction when he had tried eating pecans for the first time.

Beside her, Lane Jackson slumped in his seat with his arms crossed. His head hung low as he studied his flexing arm muscles, adoring their flawless shape.

Other students were texting under tables or doodling on their class notes.

Sighing, I rested my chin on the desk and allowed my mind to wander as Shyler argued with Mr. Craven for the next five minutes about how Mormons no longer practiced polygamy.

I found myself thinking back to the witch in the

woods. Her haunting expression was crystal clear in my mind. The memory of her was so vivid, I felt that if I reached out in front of me I would be able to touch her stone-cold face.

I pondered everything she had revealed and dissected her words. The spark had been ignited, unlocking my gift the moment I had looked into the black mirror. There was still so much to explore. I felt as if I were just scraping the surface of this inner power. The stress and burden of the unknown weighed down on the pit of my stomach.

Then there was the stranger's face behind my reflection to worry about. My mind began to question if I had indeed seen a face that day or if it was just my imagination. I contemplated the witch's caution that I would somehow be connected to others who had looked in the mirror before me. *If that was a face I saw, did they see me too? Do they know who I am and what I am capable of?*

I snapped back to reality. Apparently, Shy's heated discussion with Mr. Craven had begun to bring energy back to the classroom. She must have presented a fiery argument that humbled his disagreement.

Shyler was always untouchable when she debated. No matter who it was she argued with, if it was something she felt passionate enough to defend, you could bet your life she had enough foundation of information to knock you on your backside.

"All right, everyone, settle down. We're changing subjects!" Mr. Craven shouted to regain control of the class. "Open to page 238, and Addison, will you PLEASE stop snapping your gum? You sound like my kids playing with a huge package of bubble wrap!"

When I opened to the chapter, the pages greeted me with a sketch of an old scale. Two flat plates balanced side by side on golden chains hooked to a long beam.

What Is Karma?
Understanding the Law of Cause and Effect

"Rylee, will you start at the third paragraph and read out loud for the class?" Mr. Craven asked, glancing in my direction. I pulled the book closer to my face and quietly cleared my throat before I began reading.

"Every action we take toward others is believed to be accompanied with a generated force of energy. Whether positive or negative, the fruits of our karma match our actions with justified consequences.

"One who brings kindness and happiness to others is later rewarded with happiness and vice versa.

"There are believed to be different categories of karma. Sometimes karma is not experienced in this lifetime and may affect one's setting and circumstances once they have been reincarnated in a future life. However, Immediately Effective Karma may be reaped in one's current state and life."

The words stood out boldly as the rest of the page dissolved into blankness. I repeated the words in my mind: *Immediately Effective Karma.*

I turned to Shyler. I could tell from her expression that she also recognized the connecting dots. Is *this* what my ability was linked to? Could I be a vessel and doorway for the forces of karma?

It didn't make any sense on one hand, yet it seemed perfectly fitting on the other. Perhaps I had the ability to tamper with everyone's personal karma, at least when their actions were directed at me.

There was a loud buzz over the intercom: "Will Mr. Craven report to the main office, please?"

Craven set down his book and grabbed a stack of papers from the top of his desk and began passing them out.

"While I'm gone, everyone can start working on these worksheets. You should be able to find the answers throughout the chapter. I'll be back in a couple of minutes."

As he left and shut the door, the silence of the classroom transitioned into a loud uproar of social chattering.

Shyler leaned in beside my desk. "Could this have to do with your good luck?"

Lane glanced over from his seat on the opposite side of me. Shyler's question seemed to catch his attention.

"Whose good luck?" he asked as he shifted his torso toward our conversation. His sun-bleached bangs were slicked back in a smooth, gelled wave. The smell of his cologne mixed with his egotistic personality formed a cloud of arrogance that gravitated in our direction and made me want to choke.

"Nothing. She didn't mean anything," I said, impatiently. I grabbed my chair and positioned it to the side so my back turned to Lane, cutting him out of our conversation. I leaned in closer to Shyler and lowered my voice to avoid drawing any more attention to our confidential discussion.

"You don't believe in karma or any of that stuff, right?" I whispered.

She contemplated my question deeply. I could see in her eyes her mind opening as she reasoned with the information.

She opened her mouth. "*I believe*," she began, "in some form or way, we will be judged for all our actions, and theological measures of justice will take place."

She paused for a minute and looked down at the textbook, tracing the pictures and text with the tip of her finger.

"I *also* believe that we are very small, and there are things bigger than us that we may never understand in this life." Her eyes shot up and looked at me with excitement as she attempted to piece her thoughts together. "*And*

I believe in miracles and events taking place that don't scientifically make sense. So, why not!? Why couldn't you be in tune with some energy of justice or karma that no one else around you has the ability to tap into?"

I smiled. Shyler had a way of making the weird and unknown sound so logical, and I fed off her calmness to try to keep myself from worrying.

"Wait! You have magic karma powers?!" Lane interrupted from behind me. *Crap.* I thought he had stopped listening.

"Yeah," Shyler laughed. "Try hitting her on the back of the head. I learned that the hard way." She stared with puppy-love eyes at Lane's lovely face.

"Shyler!" I said. "Can you please not?"

The last thing I wanted was someone like Lane Jackson knowing about what was going on with my personal struggles of overcoming bewitched inner powers.

"Hold up, hold up." Lane put his hand to his mouth and pushed together his stumbling thoughts. "I've got this killer knot in my neck and shoulders. So, physically, if I give you a pleasant back massage right now, I should be able to feel it too, right? Immediate karma!" He put his hands on my shoulders without invitation and began digging his fingers into my skin.

"Yeah, I don't think it works that way," I said, feeling annoyed. His contact pestered me like an obnoxious mosquito I wished I could shoo away. Lane continued rubbing and closed his eyes.

Shyler giggled and began writing in her worksheet. In the corner of my eye I saw Addison turn in our direction, clearly irritated by the lack of attention she was receiving from Lane.

Mr. Craven walked back inside and spoke up above the chatter to settle down the class.

"All right everyone, party's over," he shouted. "What is this? A massage train? Have you even started that worksheet, Mr. Jackson?"

Mr. Craven took his hands and began kneading into Lane's shoulders like a clump of pizza dough. Lane opened his eyes and shot up in surprise.

"Argh! Craves! You're oogin' me out!"

The class laughed as a look of disgust showed in Lane's expression. Tears formed in our eyes as Shyler and I shook from silent laughter. The kind that aches deep in your belly.

I glanced once more in Lane's direction and my mood suddenly changed as he shot back a distrusting glare. Quickly, I broke eye contact and turned away, nearly pressing my cheek into my shoulder to avoid him. I could still feel his eyes burning into the back of my skull. There was no telling what was going on inside of Lane's mind. Whatever it might be, I hoped I could rely on him to not tell anyone else.

"Hey, Shy, can I get a ride home again today? Looks like my car's still in the shop," I asked as the school bell chimed down the hallway.

I guess it wasn't technically *my* car. It had been given to the family after my grandma passed away. Since it wasn't doing anything useful collecting dust in the driveway, I claimed it the second I had earned my driver's license. As old and "grandma-looking" as it was, I loved it like my baby.

"Sure, Rylee, but student council has to help clean up the gym from the assembly so I might be a while," Shyler answered. "That foam wrestling with the mascot was a big hit, right? Totally my idea. It took me two straight weeks of harassing O'Connors to finally get it okayed."

Determination and persistence; two other very strong characteristics that Shyler possessed.

"No worries. I'll try and catch up on some homework while I wait. Thanks again."

I stepped outside for some fresh air and dropped my bag at my feet. Leaning back against the building, I pressed all my body weight to the wall and slid down slowly to a comfortable sitting position. My eyes closed for a moment as I let the warm sunshine soak into my face.

Down beside my sneaker I spotted a wiggling beetle turned upside down on its fat back shell. Its klutzy legs scrambled frantically through the air, in comical need of assistance. Using the plastic tip of my shoelace, I gently nudged it onto its feet and watched it scuttle away into a nearby crack in the sidewalk.

"Hey, stranger."

I flattened my hand above my eyes like a visor to block the blinding sun. Through the glaring outline of a silhouette shadow I was able to recognize Merritt's tall frame. Delight fluttered inside my chest. Just being in his presence intoxicated me with joy.

"Are you waiting for a ride?" he asked.

"Oh, yeah. Shyler's taking me home in a while. I'm just killing time." I smoothed out the waves in my shirt to keep my hands from fidgeting with nervousness.

"I can take you now so she doesn't have to drive out of her way. You live right by me." The logical tone in his voice gave me no choice in the matter and he practically dragged me over to his parking spot.

We approached his truck just as Shyler walked out of the gym doors. As she spotted me with Merritt she smiled. I gave her a silent wave and she returned it with a wink and a nod.

From our lifetime of friendship, it was easy to translate

her body language: "Next time I see you, you *will* be required to tell me every juicy detail."

I blushed on the inside and tried to act naturally like I didn't notice her wink.

Merritt's truck had the aroma of new leather and mint aftershave. Just like him, it smelled absolutely fantastic. He tossed his beanie in the corner of the window as he switched on the engine and reached down to the gearshift, pulling it into reverse.

Merritt was so mesmerizing, which deeply intimidated me, but I faked my confidence and tried starting a conversation.

"My dad promised he'd teach me to drive stick this year."

Something about piloting stick shift seemed so thrilling to me. I couldn't wait to feel like the fast speed racers in the movies that spun out every time they wanted to make a grand exit. I could picture myself drifting around sharp corners and cutting cookies in an open field.

"Well, if your dad never gets around to it, give me a call and I'll teach you," Merritt said.

"Will you teach me donuts?"

"Absolutely mandatory."

The feelings of nervousness and intimidation suddenly faded away. When I talked to Merritt, it felt like we had never been apart and we were once again childhood playmates. The chemistry jumped right back in where it had left off, and I surprisingly found myself more comfortable around him than almost anyone I knew.

"So, when I push down on the clutch I'm free to change the gears. Go ahead and try changing it to third," he directed me.

I grabbed the stick and attempted to pull, but it wouldn't budge.

"Like this," he dropped his hand on top of mine and

guided me to the right gear. My mind froze for half a second from his soft touch. Then I quickly gathered my thoughts.

"Ah, yes, up and then over. I guess I can't just yank it straight across, can I?"

After that, I got the hang of it and didn't need his help anymore. I supposed if I were wiser I could have acted stupid so he would keep holding my hand. Alas, I never thought of these clever things until after they took place.

We pulled up to the driveway and saw my mom walking back inside from her stroll to the mailbox. Merritt waved to her as I reached down for my book bag.

"Thank you so much for the ride. I'll see you around."

"Anytime, Ry. See you at school." Then he flashed me a quick grin.

I bit my lip as I turned to unbuckle my seatbelt. With that one smile my wall of self-confidence was shattered again, and I felt weak and vulnerable in his unblemished presence. I had to hold my breath and look away to keep from displaying my pathetic infatuation.

I stepped out and allowed my nerves to settle while I watched him leave. As I turned back and walked up to the front door I looked down at my hands and held them together, trying to reenact the way he had held onto mine just moments before.

Suddenly, I felt my cell phone vibrate. Two missed calls from Shyler. I smiled to myself. It looked like I had some explaining to do.

Chapter 7

Will anyone be having dessert tonight, ladies?"
My mom looked kindly into the eyes of our young waiter and smiled, "We'll go ahead and split a piece of that delicious coconut crème pie you mentioned earlier, if you don't mind."

She was kind to everyone. Whether it was the stranger at the grocery store, the homeless man collecting cans, or the traffic controller directing the passing cars.

After our waiter left the table, we jumped right back into our conversation.

"Was that Merritt I saw dropping you off this afternoon? Looks like he's all grown up." She smiled at me and raised her eyebrows.

"Ha! Yeah. He's, um . . . grown up . . . and completely gorgeous," I added.

We both giggled as a huge plate of pie was brought and set between us on the table. The waiter set the check next to Mom, and I watched *Evelyn Perry* artistically dance in ink across the signature line.

The light flavor of cream pie tingled my taste buds. It was the perfect companion to compliment my meal and settled nicely into my already stretched out stomach, just enough to feel past full without getting sick.

Mom's eyes changed.

"Rylee, there's something I wanted to talk to you about. It's actually why I brought you with me to dinner tonight." Her serious tone seemed unusual. My mind stirred with curiosity and I wondered for a moment if this had anything to do with my hidden secret. I swallowed hard.

"I haven't been feeling well lately and went to the doctor to get a couple of tests," she began.

I didn't like where this conversation was heading. A cold chill went up my arms and my spine. My throat began to feel dry and I reached for my water glass.

She took a deep breath and looked straight into my eyes.

"The results came back with some bad news." She paused for a second and slowly exhaled. I could hear her voice tremble as she attempted to speak with confidence to make everything sound under control. "They found a brain tumor, Rylee."

My emotions shut down. It was as if all of my feelings suddenly washed out and drained like an open sink plug, leaving my insides dry. I felt nothing.

"The doctor said . . ." Mom's mouth continued moving, but the words wouldn't translate inside my eardrums. Everything became muted around me, and my eyes shifted to see if anyone else in the room was experiencing the same silence. The moment was being pulled and stretched by both sides expanding and slowing down time in front of my eyes.

I studied my mother's facial expression. Tears began rolling down her cheeks, but still nothing would register inside of me. The deafness turned to high pitched ringing in my ears, and I lost all memory of the rest of our conversation.

My next recollection was of the two of us driving home. Our silence was drowned out by the soft humming of the car engine. I leaned against the window and gazed at the flickering streetlights. Red, yellow, and green danced across the window in morphed reflections.

Mom reached into the side compartment of the driver's seat and pulled out an orange pack of gum.

"Want one?"

She snatched a stick for her and tossed the package across the seat to me. I grabbed a piece reluctantly and dropped it on my tongue. The sweet taste awoke and energized my gloomy mind.

"Wanna pick a radio station?" she asked as she turned on the speakers. I could tell the silence was making her uneasy.

Reaching forward, I twisted the tuning knob until it connected with my favorite channel. We listened as the radio DJ announced raffle winners for an upcoming weekend concert.

I laughed under my breath.

"What's so funny?" Mom asked.

"This radio host sounds like a tool. He seems pretty cocky for a man whose only friends are the fourteen-year-old girls that listen to his station."

She laughed back. "What are you talking about?"

We listened as the announcer transitioned to the next track. "All right, Trishell, have fun at next week's concert! If you need a date, don't hesitate to give me a call. I'll play a song recently released from the latest album just to get you feeling the heat! This is J-Dog Jacie and thanks for listening!"

We both started laughing. *J-Dog Jacie.* Of course his name was as ridiculous as J-Dog Jacie.

As the lyrics started playing, Mom began to sing along. I looked over at her, surprised.

"Mom! How do you know this song?" I asked, shocked and a little impressed.

"I don't know! Harrison taught it to me the other day." We both laughed and sang along. As the music clouded with rhythm and noise, our spirits rose. I turned up the volume and we danced to the hard bass, caught up in the melody. We pulled down our hair and began bobbing our heads like idolized rock stars.

For a small second, we were free from the recent news of cancer. It didn't exist. Not here, not while we were dancing.

"Why don't you sing more?!" Mom laughed. "Your voice is so beautiful. I wish you would audition for a choir solo one of these days."

"You're my mom. You have to say that."

"I mean it! I want to hear you sing at the next choir concert," she insisted.

I rolled my eyes and turned up the music volume even higher to end the conversation.

Grabbing her water bottle, Mom began singing into her imaginary microphone. She squeezed the sides and the slightly loose bottle cap flew into the air, hitting the ceiling as water poured out all down her seat and pants.

I roared with laughter and she tried to wipe the blissful tears in her eyes to keep from crashing off the side of the road.

I never wanted to forget this moment. My heart soaked up every detail into my memory to store for a rainy day. I wanted to remember the happiness, the laughter, the music pounding in my ears, the taste of Mom's tropical gum, and the glowing street lights guiding us through the darkness and erasing the pain of bad news.

Right then, being there with Mom, was a moment in time I bookmarked to always treasure for years to come.

Lying in bed that night, the happiness of the car ride began to fade and my mind was attacked with worries of Mom's new health discovery. Haunting questions began seeping into my mind. *How bad is it? What if she doesn't get better? How long until she . . . ?*

I tore the bed covers off my body and blindly stumbled through the dark house into the cold bathroom. Without switching on the lights, I turned on the shower as hot as I could stand it, threw my pile of clothes on the bathroom rug, and climbed inside.

The steam from the shower danced with the freezing air of the open window above me. In the darkness I could focus on the sensation of the scorching water warming my skin and the outside air cooling the inside of my lungs. As the light of the stars began to trickle into the room, my eyes adjusted and I could see the fog of my breath leach out into the mist.

Holding to the sides of the tub, I lowered myself to the ground. I sat and leaned against the cool tiles and closed my eyes while the water ran through my ratted, wet hair.

I concentrated on breathing and felt my chest slowly rise and deflate over and over again. The sliding air soothed the surface of my warm throat and steadied my faint heartbeat.

I wouldn't let this pull me down. *Mom will be fine*, I told myself. I had nothing to fear. And I blocked out the panic of her sickness.

My head began bobbing to the side, and I caught myself drifting to sleep. I turned off the shower, wrapped myself in a towel, and slipped back into bed. My pillow, scented with calming lavender, perfectly cupped the side of my face and every muscle in my body relaxed and molded into the bedding. I sighed and let the lingering warmth from the hot shower carry me away into sleep.

Chapter 8

After ending a dismal day of school, a sprinkle of happiness greeted me as I walked out to the parking lot with Shyler. My dad had surprised me by dropping off the car while I was in class so I could finally drive myself home again.

My mind was exhausted from spending the entire day pushing Mom's bad news away from the focal point of my thoughts. Seeing the car brought an optimistic light that distracted me from the day's shadowy pessimism.

"I guess I don't need a ride anymore, Shy. I'll see you Monday," I said as I cheerfully bounced my way towards my parking spot.

While waiting for the engine to warm up, I began readjusting everything Dad had changed while driving it. To let my feet comfortably reach the pedals, I slid the seat forward then tipped down the rearview mirror back to eye level. I synced the speakers to my music so I didn't have to bore myself with the rambling sports plays of AM radio.

As I pulled down the sun visor, a crinkled note fell into my lap. I smoothed out the corners and read the message.

Sweep the back porch.
−Dad

I laughed and nudged the paper between the cracks of the vent so I wouldn't forget.

When I had almost reached home, I approached the turn that led directly to Merritt's house. His face centered in the spotlight of my thoughts where I couldn't shake him away. I pictured his bright eyes that lit up when he smiled. He had somehow become my fuel for daily survival, and it was difficult to function until my tank was refilled.

At the last second, I changed my destination and made my way toward his driveway. I had hoped to have more time to come up with an excuse for the surprise visit but was suddenly caught off guard when I spotted him outside in his front yard. The thought prodded my mind to hurry and turn back, but he had already seen me coming. I realized I needed a plan quickly.

"Hey, stranger!" Merritt called out as I parked in the side gravel. "What brings you to this side of the neighborhood?" He was hosing the soap off his freshly washed pickup truck.

My mind worked quickly as I walked up to greet him. Seeing his truck presented me with a brilliant idea.

"Are you busy this afternoon?" I asked, pulling my ponytail to one side of my shoulder. My hands stumbled over one another as I continuously brushed my fingers through the thick cluster of hair over and over again. He rested his elbows on the roof of the truck.

"I'm completely free," he responded.

"If it's not too much trouble, I was wondering if I could still take you up on that offer to teach me to drive stick. Maybe around the parking lot of the food market or something?"

His classic, charming smile slid across his face. He seemed happy about my interest in his personal tutoring.

"I'd love to," he replied. He put all his weight against the car and pushed off. Crossing his arms, he grabbed the bottom rim of his soaked grey shirt and pulled it up over his head.

For some reason I was caught off guard by the quick flash of his perfect abs. *Of course*, I thought to myself, *why wouldn't Merritt Emerson also have a perfect body to go along with his flawless smile and dreamy personality?*

He picked up the hose and started making his way toward the house.

"I'll just grab a dry shirt," he said as he walked away.

I sighed. "Oh, that's not really necessary," I mumbled under my breath. I tried saying it quietly enough so only I could hear, but suddenly Merritt chuckled and turned back toward me, triggering the hose nozzle so a quick stream of water came flying in my direction. I ducked behind the trunk and dodged its splash. After dropping the hose by the side of the house, he jogged inside.

As I waited outside, I circled around his truck lightly tracing the outlines of each window and door handle with the tips of my fingers. I peered into the backseat and noticed his small duffle bag stuffed with water bottles and a grassy pair of football cleats.

When he came back out, he wore a tight fitting white T-shirt that stenciled his unfortunately now-covered torso.

As we hopped inside the truck, he reached down into the glove box and pulled out his MP3 player.

"DJ Rylee, will you do the honors?" he said as he set it in my lap. I opened his music playlist choices and began giggling.

"Last listened to 90s Classic Love Songs?"

His smile quickly wiped off his face and he grabbed the player from my hands, staring straight ahead.

He cleared his throat.

"I am confident and comfortable with my masculinity."

I tried to hold back my smile as I stared at him. Silently, he turned on the engine and put the truck into reverse. He reached his arm up behind my headrest and turned backwards to make sure the driveway behind us was clear. I found it hard to look away from his handsome face so close to mine.

"And, yeah, sometimes I just need to jam to Savage Garden's love songs," he said defensively.

"I won't tell anyone," I whispered back to him.

I stalled the pickup three times before finally getting it to roll around the parking lot. Once the truck was moving, I was fine switching gears. It was just difficult transitioning from park to in-motion.

"Just wait until you start going up hills, then you're really in for a treat," he laughed. He was a very patient teacher. Never once did I sense judgment or frustration when I messed up. Merritt always seemed to be calm and collected, no matter the situation.

After successfully parking in every available parking spot without error, we called it a day.

"In celebration of your success, I think we deserve a treat," he said as he began walking into the market. I shut the car door and followed him inside.

We walked down the aisles until we reached the frozen section. The lights behind the glass row of doors continuously switched on and greeted us as we approached each frozen shelf. Merritt stopped at the mini buckets of ice cream and peeled open the clear door. A chill rushed out and tickled my arms, causing goose bumps to instantaneously form on my skin. I jumped to the opposite side of the door and shivered, trying to avoid the blast of cold.

Merritt pushed the door out further and turned to me

so we were perfectly separated by the cold sheet of glass. He brought his lips close to the door's surface and exhaled deeply, causing the warm steam of his breath to cloud up the vision between us. Raising his finger, he began to trace the outline of my face on his transparent chalkboard.

As flawless as Merritt seemed, I realized his drawing skills were far from impeccable. Giving up and realizing his doodling efforts were a miserable fail, he smashed his nose and puffed up cheeks against the glass, replacing his art with a giant smear of his face.

With a crooked grin, I laughed under my breath. I noticed that Merritt was opening up more and more to me, showing his true personality.

After a heated round of rock-paper-scissors, the ice cream flavor was decided, and we made our way back outside.

Merritt began feeling around in his pockets while we walked back to the truck. He paused and looked around.

"Um, you have the keys, right?" he asked, realizing his pockets were empty. My eyes opened wide as I sucked in a quick, startled breath.

"Ummmm," I responded and looked over at the locked truck. Through the window, we watched as the keys dangled in the ignition.

"Rylee, Rylee, Rylee," he reached up and hooked his arm around my neck, "What am I supposed to do with you?"

"I'm so sorry," I laughed. My hands reached up and grabbed his arm hanging over my shoulder. Even with a simple, friendly arm hold, I craved every minute Merritt and I were physically touching. It felt as though a magnetic force was layered beneath our skins and constantly reaching for one another.

He let go of me and walked over to the bed of the

truck. Dropping to his hands and knees, he rolled over onto his back and inched his way under the back wheels, so his head and shoulders were out of sight. The bottom of his shirt barely pulled up and I again caught a tiny glimpse of the skin of his stomach.

I sat puzzled and watched his feet squirm as he reached for something.

He crawled back out with a small silver box in his hand and pulled out a spare key to the truck.

"We're saved," he said and walked over to open my door for me.

"You're such a hero," I teased him and climbed into the passenger's seat. During the drive home we sat contentedly eating our delicious cake batter ice cream.

Chapter 9

"I can't believe this! A ten page essay draft, four chapters of reading, *AND* the midterm test on Monday? Mr. Craven is so frustrating!" Shyler vented, walking out of class.

"Speaking of frustration, you seemed a little fired up in that debate with Lewis today," I teased as we stopped to open our lockers.

"Lewis Mahoy is an IDIOT. He can't sit there and say to my face that Mormon's aren't Christians. Christ is the entire foundation of the LDS religion! Sounds like all those football concussions must have caused damage to his thick skull."

"You're not sounding very Christian right now," I said as we walked to her next classroom. She split from my side into the doorway then spun back and looked at me.

"No one's perfect," she said and smiled smugly.

I continued down the hallway alone and turned the corner toward the choir room. Reaching into my backpack, I lost grip of my class folder and dropped it, spreading sheet music all across the floor. *Lovely.*

"Oh, how tragic," Addison laughed as she walked up behind me. While I bent over to pick up my mess, she deliberately stepped on a huge stack of papers and twisted her boot to send more music flying away from me. I continued organizing the clutter and ignored her.

Behind me, I could hear paper shuffling and felt the presence of someone leaning over to help. I looked back to find Merritt organizing my folder.

"That was classy," he said, looking up at Addison in the distance. I stopped what I was doing and watched her walk away.

"Don't worry. I've become a strong believer in fate. All that serendipitous cause and effect power of the cosmos crap? Oh, it's real." I spoke softly enough so only he could hear me.

My eyes remained locked on Addison. Here, now, I wanted her action countered. I concentrated furiously to push out my balancing power. The invisible energy began to soak out of my skin and to swim in her direction.

Addison flipped her long hair over her shoulder and glanced back at us vainly as she began to turn the corner. She turned a moment too soon and without looking forward ran straight into the wall in front of her. Humiliated, she quickly straightened out her wardrobe and dashed away.

Merritt snorted as we tried to control our silent laughter. The hallway began crowding with more and more students leaving class. I leaned my weight against a nearby locker to push myself up off the ground.

"How's it going, Karma?" Lane suddenly walked up behind me and whispered in my ear as he passed down the hall. He eyed me with a strange fascination, clearly amused by his discovery of my hidden secret days earlier.

He exchanged glances with Merritt and tipped his head, grinning while he walked away. I glared in Lane's direction as he disappeared.

"What was that about?" Merritt asked.

"Nothing," I quickly replied. "Thanks for your help, I better head to class."

Our hands lightly brushed as he handed me the collection of loose papers. I watched Merritt quickly attempt to wipe away a hidden smile that appeared with the sudden physical contact.

" 'Kay, bye," I laughed and spun around to hide my blushing face. As I walked away I sneaked in a quick glance behind me once more to find Merritt looking back as well. We laughed when we both caught each other's simultaneous double take. Merritt reached up with his textbook in his hand and with one loose finger scratched behind his neck and played with his dark curls.

I paused at my classroom door and sighed, trying to collect my butterfly thoughts before returning back to reality.

"No, no, no. Stop, everyone, stop." Mr. Luke silenced the choir of voices as we attempted to polish our newest song ballad. "Altos, you keep sounding flat at measure thirty, and there's someone in the second soprano section that's way too overpowering. Take it down a notch."

Although his words were direct, Mr. Luke always had a soft, patient tone as he taught. "You ladies need to listen to each other. It's the balance of blending that creates your beautiful sound."

He paused and thought for a minute.

Mr. Luke's short, chestnut-brown hair beautifully complemented his matching skin tone. His dark goatee always looked freshly trimmed and perfectly stenciled his rounded lips.

"I want you ladies to visualize something for me a moment." He walked to his desk and pulled out a chair.

After dragging it back to the middle of the room, he twirled it around and sat straddling the back, leaning his folded arms against the headrest. The tips of his dark, dry elbows peeked out underneath his white, rolled up sleeves.

"Imagine you're holding in your hands a giant pot of delicious, golden honey," he said. Some of the girls giggled and playfully opened their arms, hugging the invisible honey jars sitting in their laps.

"Think about its thickness and richness. Now, close your eyes and slowly stir the honey."

I looked to my left and then over to my right. Down the rows of chairs, I watched hands of imaginary honey dippers stirring in unison.

Mr. Luke spoke in his calm, baritone voice, "Think about how the honey forms together into one big whole, how it reshapes and molds into its surroundings. It blends with itself as a single energy."

We meditated in silence as we took in his soothing words.

Mr. Luke rose out of his chair and quietly stepped over to his abandoned music stand. Without a word he raised his hands in the air and began swaying his arms to the leading tempo.

We opened our mouths and listened as our voices transformed into a single sound, and we became one. The angelic chords blended into a serene melody, and I began to truly recognize the beauty and power of balance.

Chapter 10

"Two hot chocolates, two nachos, one of those licorice rope guys, aaaaaaand what else do you want?"

"Shyler! You're eating the entire snack shack, Fatty! Settle down!"

The only reason I could get away with calling my best friend fat was because she was probably the skinniest girl at school. She had a tall, slender frame and got away with eating absolutely anything she wanted.

"It's in the genes," she would always justify. "My dad was 6'6" in high school and skinnier than me. I was just gifted with his crazy metabolism." Even with her justification, it was hard for me to grasp so much food fitting into such a tiny structure.

We squeezed into the front seats of the stadium's student section right below the band. It was impossible to hear anything with the loud drumming and constant cheers of howling students. The Lava Bears were beating Stevenson 21 to 14 in the third quarter of the game, and Bears had possession.

I leaned to the side trying to spot Merritt through the busy jersey numbers huddled below the stands. On the dry grassy field, a tall player jogged to the bench and unbuckled his helmet. As he effortlessly pulled it off, steam rose from his wet hair as it mixed with the cold autumn weather. He turned in my direction, lifted his hand, and smiled.

"Merritt," I chuckled under my breath and waved back.

"Oh, hi, are you even listening to me?" Shyler's interruption zoned me back into the conversation that was apparently taking place beside me. "I said Lane just texted me asking what we're doing after the game."

As I tried to stay focused on Shyler's words, my eyes couldn't help but remain glued to Merritt's football jersey. "Isn't he supposed to be focused on playing? Not texting you from the field?" I said.

"Quarterbacks don't play defense, dork. He's sitting on the bench. Can we please focus on the fact that I just received a text from Lane Jackson?" It appeared her crush with Lane was growing day by day.

Just then the crowd roared and jumped to their feet as our team intercepted and ran for the end zone. The stadium echoed in enthusiasm as the announcer screamed, "TOUCHDOWN BULLDOGS!"

The plays faded together as the teams juggled the football back and forth across the field. I glanced up, reviewing the scoreboard, and before I knew it we were in the final minutes of the last quarter, and Bulldogs were barely losing. I felt my pocket ringing and pulled out my phone.

"It's my mom. I'll be right back. Mom? Mom! Can't hear you! Give me a second. I'm going somewhere quieter." I stood up and tiptoed sideways along the edge of cheering students until I reached the outside steps. Behind the bleachers I found an isolated hideout and held up the phone. "Is everything all right?"

"Just checking in. Sounds like you're having fun,

I'm sorry to pull you away." Mom's calm voice traveled through my ears the way the ocean breeze slipped through a hollow seashell.

"You're fine. I don't mind. You're sure everything's okay?" I replied. Hearing the concern in my own voice, I realized that I had become overly protective with her.

"Yeah. Just . . . Be safe tonight, honey." Her voice paused for a brief moment. "I just felt like I needed to call you. Please be safe tonight."

"Thanks, Mom. Besides flying footballs, I don't think I'm in much danger at the game. Love you."

I hung up and casually walked back toward the stands. When I looked up at the unappealing benches of crowded students, I decided to stay put and watch the game from ground level. I leaned against the fence and squinted at the scoreboard.

VISITORS: 30 HOME: 28

The game was seconds from being over, and I watched Merritt run out onto the field. I began calculating the possible score outcomes of the next game play. If he were to kick and score this field goal, our school would win.

I watched him shake his fingers at his sides and jump in place to keep his muscles warm. He scanned the fence line and spotted me standing alone. Trying to help ease his anxiety, all I could think to do was give a quick, corny two thumbs up. He nodded and turned back facing the goal post. *Ha! I'm such a dork. Thumbs up? Really?*

As the play began and the football was tossed back, the player on his knee positioned the ball into place. The posture of his crouched body reminded me of Merritt earlier that day kneeling down to help me pick up my papers.

Please let him make this, I thought to myself. *He was kind to me today. If there is anything inside me that could help him right now, please let it support him.*

I visualized the balancing scale that illustrated my internal gift. Thinking of Merritt and how much good swelled inside of him, how much of that goodness he had directed toward me, I had to open that doorway of symmetry that would aim good luck back in his direction.

Please, please make this! I concentrated with extreme intensity.

While the different colors of jerseys tangled together, Merritt kicked hard and the ball flew through the air. I held my breath and watched. It seemed to travel in slow motion as the ball spun and soared perfectly through the center of the goal posts.

The refs shot their hands straight into the air as the stadium howled. Blue jerseys jumped and tackled Merritt in celebration, and I couldn't help but scream with joy from the lonely fence line.

"Yes! Look who finally decided to show up!" Lane was sitting against a tree stump, surrounded by his classmates and a few football players from the team. The light of the bonfire lightly stenciled his shadowed profile. Besides his voice, it was the only thing that made him recognizable.

"Great game tonight, Lane!" Shyler yelled as we made our way closer to the crowd. I scanned the silhouettes hoping to find Merritt or at least another friendly face, but to my disappointment all the eyes staring back at me sent out a clear message that Shyler and I were not welcome.

"Oh joy, look who decided to crash the party," Addison muttered, followed by a chorus of giggling from her mob of admirers.

Shyler, ignoring the friendless vibes that floated through the air, made herself at home finding a seat as close to Lane as possible. I quickly grabbed my cell phone and looked down at the screen, pretending to be busy to avoid starting a conversation with anyone nearby. I was ready to go home immediately.

Lane began reaching into a nearby cooler when Shyler spoke out before he could offer us anything.

"Don't bother, Lane. We're not drinking."

"Would hate to put a mark on your perfect, churchy record," Addison taunted. "How about a cup of coffee? Oh wait, that won't do either . . . Um, apple juice? In a sippy cup, perhaps?"

The friends surrounding her began to snicker. *Ugh! I can't stand that girl!* As I glared at her and held my breath, I tried to focus on unleashing a fresh dish of karma. There was emptiness inside. I pushed again but nothing happened.

Then I pieced together the obvious. Addison's insults were directed to Shyler, not to me. No matter how hard I tried, my power couldn't do anything in this situation.

The night carried on with a variety of gossiping, one-upping, and detailed replays of the evening's game. After listening to Lewis Mahoy's third fictional story about getting into fistfights with college students, I had to get out of there.

Discreetly, I sneaked away from the fire and explored a little pathway that led to a secluded area in the woods where I was safe from the toxic noise of the party. I took in a deep breath, enjoying the cool air and thick silence of the blended trees.

Just then my phone chimed.

Text from Merritt: "Hey, how's your night going?"

I couldn't stop the smile that escaped my lips when I saw his name. I replied, "Somehow got dragged to Lane's bonfire party. Now I'm hiding. Had to get away from all those puffed-up egos."

Suddenly, I heard what sounded like a branch snapping from behind a tree in the distance. I turned and saw nothing. Probably just another raccoon enhancing my jittery imagination.

I glanced at my phone again. New text message: "Ha! What a coincidence! I just got—"

"Rylee!" I jumped and looked up before I could finish reading.

Lane inched his way toward me from the trees in the distance. For some reason the sight of him outside the usual school atmosphere gave off a more exposed complexion than I was used to seeing.

"I thought I saw you wandering out here. Not having fun yet?" He reached up and feathered his stiff, wavy bangs.

I rolled my eyes.

"Oh no, having a blast."

Something about Lane made me uneasy, besides his eavesdropping and stumbling upon my secret during class. It was something hiding behind his expression that I didn't trust. My senses began twitching inside of me.

The leaves crunched under his feet as he came closer. He tilted his head to the side and rubbed the muscles between the corner of his neck and shoulder.

"I'm glad you came tonight, Rylee. I was really hoping you would."

I thought for a moment, puzzled. *What is he talking about? Why in the world would he care whether I came or not?* I took a step backwards and felt the back of my shirt brush against a stiff tree.

"Thanks, I guess? I just came because Shyler wanted to come." I tried to sound friendly but without giving him any impression that I had any interest or desire to be there.

He continued walking closer and closer. Too close. All too soon I found myself trapped between him and the tree. Even then, I kept expecting him to stop, but he continued moving forward until his entire body frame came onto me.

His sudden contact completely caught me off guard.

"Wow! Um, hi. I need to go."

I tried taking a step to the side when he pushed me back, pinning me against the tree. His strong hands clung tightly to my arms below my shoulders. I immediately started struggling to get free.

"Lane! Stop it! Let go now!"

He pressed his weight against me and covered my mouth to hush my cries.

"Just hear me out for a sec, okay? I was thinking about your little supernatural karma deal, and I came up with this plan."

Our faces were so close that his nose pressed against my cheek. While he attempted to calm me down, I could smell alcohol and feel his breath touch my lips as he spoke. I struggled and tried using all of my energy to break through his hold, but every ounce of effort hardly made him budge. My limber structure was no match for his powerful physique.

"When someone causes you pain, their pain is amplified, am I correct?"

I looked up at his face as I tried to push him away. He still wore the same hidden expression that made my nerves cringe.

"So, simple math suggests that causing pleasure should work the same way. Brilliant, right? I help you out, you help me. I think we've got ourselves a win-win situation here," he explained.

I felt nauseated. He reached below my shirt and traced his fingers along the lining of my belt and my bare stomach. Ever since the little friendly back massage in class, he must have been plotting a way to boost the circumstances with me. My blood immediately began to boil with anger.

I can NOT let this happen, I thought to myself. Before he could succeed, I would fight and scrape out every last drop of effort inside of me to make him quit. There had to be some form of Karma that could attack Lane in our surroundings!

I quickly opened my mouth and bit down on two of his fingers as hard as I possibly could.

"OW!" he yelled, "Seriously?! You little—"

Suddenly, I watched someone else's hand reach over and grab Lane's shoulder, rapidly spinning him backwards. The action followed with a loud CRACK!

In my state of shock everything happened in a flash. The last thing I remembered seeing was Merritt with his hand clenched in a fist and Lane stumbling to the ground, holding his bleeding nose in the palms of his hands.

"Leaving right now would probably be a very wise decision." He was looking straight at me, but I knew Merritt's advice was directed to Lane.

I suddenly tasted blood and realized that as I had bitten Lane's fingers, I had also sunk my teeth into the side of my cheek. While it had happened I had been too distracted to notice, but now I felt the pain throbbing in my mouth.

Hiding the tears in his eyes, Lane shot up and ran back up the trail as fast as he could. We were left alone in the silence of the trees.

Merritt cautiously took a step toward me and asked if I was all right. By the time I had gathered all of my thoughts, collecting what had just happened, I realized I was trembling.

Without saying a word I leapt straight into Merritt's arms. He held me and rested his chin on the top of my head. With one hand he reached up to support my neck with his fingers tangled in my hair.

"Rylee! I've been looking for you everywhere! What happened to Lane's face? What's going on?" Shyler shouted as she came through the trees. When she found the two of us, I was still trembling.

Chapter 11

Can we hurry it up over there!? I don't have time for this today! And, by the way, you're out of napkins. Very professional."

I don't have time for you either today, Mr. Kestler. Most days I'm able to take his nasty attitude, but today I didn't exactly feel like being hassled. I had a horrible night and had no desire to spend this afternoon feeling just as awful. *What is he doing here on a Saturday anyway? He never gets coffee on Saturdays.*

As I slammed his latte cup down, a little puddle of cream splashed onto the counter. Mr. K eyed me angrily. The skin beneath the dark spots on his face began to simmer red.

"Do you have any idea how much money this suit cost me? If you'd have spilled even a DROP on it, I would have had this company pay for a new one!"

I didn't say anything. I could feel the warmth in my neck and cheeks as I tried not to concentrate on how much I hated him right now. Behind my tightened lips, my tongue curled to the side, kneading the bite mark in my cheek from fighting Lane.

Inside of me, I felt my powers of karma boil, fighting

to escape my self-control. I wanted him to be punished, but I fought off the energy. Avoiding eye contact, I rang up his order at the register and handed him his change.

"Congratulations. My four-year-old could have made this coffee better than you," he said.

My patience couldn't take it anymore. I let go of my inner power's restraints and felt it seep out of my body. Taking a deep, deep breath, I looked him straight in the eyes. Then I smiled.

"You have a *wonderful* day, Mr. Kestler."

As he clutched the receipt in my hand, I held to it tightly without loosening my grip. He looked up at me, slightly confused by my reaction. I felt a warm blanket of justice begin to flow over me. With a playful wink, I gracefully let go of the piece of paper.

At that exact moment there was a sudden, loud crash outside of the shop. Everyone immediately stood and looked out the big, glass windows searching for the source of the ear-splitting noise.

"MY CAR!" Mr. Kestler screamed.

In the parking lot, Mr. K's Corvette had rolled down the curb and crashed into the back of a nearby police vehicle.

He glanced back at me and noticed my smile remained firmly carved into my cheekbones. Baffled and shocked, he didn't have time to process my reaction and ran outside.

The sheriff hopped out circling the car. Even from indoors, everyone could clearly process the conversation that was taking place in the parking lot.

"I swear I had my emergency brake on, sheriff! What happened just now was impossible!" he apologized.

For the years of spitting fire I had always observed accompanying Mr. K, I was surprised by how upset and genuinely crushed he looked as he stood next to his damaged car. For a split second, an unexpected wave of guilt pressed on the back of my mind for causing this to happen. I quickly brushed it away.

He deserves it, I rationalized. *It all balances out, Mr. Kestler. Sometimes your actions just might come back to bite you.*

The next morning was a cowgirl hat kind of day. My hair draped in big curls that covered my shoulders, and I wore my cornflower blue, lace tank top with layers of beads and ribbons. My eyes were outlined in bright blue liner that made my spirit feel alive and refreshed.

I was feeling better today. The sun was bright and clear, warming up the morning, and I figured I could take advantage of my free Sunday by spending some time outdoors.

On the entryway table I found a stack of stamped envelopes that my dad had forgotten to mail the day before and walked them to the mailbox. At the end of the dirt road I stalled as I caught the corner of Merritt's home over the tall treetops.

Although our houses were close, the connecting road bent through the acres of trees, taking extra time to loop around and drive a car into his long driveway. As a kid, I found it easier and faster to run and cut through the back wood lots when I'd go over to play.

I casually dropped the letters into the square post box one by one, soaking in the beauty of the fresh day.

Standing clear of the shade produced the perfect temperature as the sunshine heated my skin. I listened to the cheerful birds whistling their daily greetings to the surrounding treetops. The wildflowers against the side of the road were decorated with white wings of fluttering butterflies. I watched one explore in the distance as its little body clumsily flopped from one bush to the next.

"Rylee!" I heard Merritt's voice off in the distance as he rushed down the road to catch me. He wore a casual plaid shirt rolled up to his elbows and lightly faded jeans that fell straight at his waist, flattering his form.

"C'mere! I want to show you something."

As if the sunshine wasn't bright enough, seeing Merritt lit up everything further in the surrounding air. I finished mailing the remaining envelopes and rushed to greet him.

He watched me closely as I approached him. "You look lovely this fine morning."

"Yeah, you don't look too bad yourself."

I leaned sideways into him with a flirting nudge. We began to walk through the thick trees that led out away from the nearby properties.

With Merritt here I couldn't be happier, but seeing his face suddenly brought back the painful memories from the bonfire. A shiver climbed and tickled the sides of my arms. I felt sick and repulsed as I played back the scene in my mind.

"I haven't had the chance to thank you, Merritt, for the other night with Lane. If you hadn't been there . . ."

"Don't worry about it," he cut me off. I was glad he did. Neither of us wanted to think about what could have happened if he hadn't shown up. I shook my head and tried to escape the tormenting thought.

"Haven't punched anyone in a while anyways and I was starting to get bored," he teased after a moment had passed.

I laughed. "When was the last time you punched someone?" He smiled and put his hands in his pockets.

"Oh, probably Spencer Nielson," he confessed, nonchalantly.

"Spencer Nielson? From second grade?!"

He quickly defended himself, "He kept trying to steal my skeleton pog slammer. Do you have any idea how valuable that thing was?"

"Pog slammers? Really, Merritt? Didn't those things go out of style before we were even born?" I asked, giggling.

I reached up and ruffled his hair. Perhaps it was the cowgirl hat, but for some reason I was feeling extra bold today. I was trying to filter and control the intimidation that usually flowed when I was around Merritt.

His eyes flashed over at me with a mischievous expression.

"Speaking of childhood . . ." He took a quick step back and put his hands over my eyes. "Keep walking and I'll show you the surprise."

I reached forward, stepping blindly with big, over-exaggerated movements to make sure there was nothing I could trip over. I laughed to myself as my inaccurate equilibrium caused me to teeter totter back and forth with each visionless step. While I cautiously followed his verbal directions and guiding hands, he came to a sudden stop and uncovered my eyes.

I was flooded with dozens of long-forgotten childhood memories as I faced the old tree house fort we had built together when we were little.

"No way!" I yelled. Merritt smiled and led me to the bottom of the stepladder.

I was surprised by the smallness of the stairs that I had struggled to reach years earlier. The wood creaked and moaned as I slowly put weight on each climbing step. I pulled myself inside the fort and scooted across the floor-boards to make room for both of us to fit.

When Merritt joined me, he leaned back resting his weight against his elbows on the floor.

The fort seemed lonely and pressed a faint ache against

my heart. The ground was sprinkled in dust and dirty pine needles that had fallen through the roof cracks. Cobwebs decorated the ceiling corners, and an old, torn quilt lay bunched on the side of the room covered in leaves and loose cotton.

I could almost hear the torn blanket crying out in sickness, shriveled from its state of neglect and loneliness. My mother's health and despicable tumor traveled into my mind, and I pictured it tearing her insides apart like the cloth of cotton.

My head shook to escape the thought as I searched to find something else to focus on.

"It looks so different now," I said, taking in the setting.

Merritt reached for a rusty tin bucket lying on its side next to the window. He turned it over and examined the inside.

"I remember you dropping water balloons on me from this window!" he suddenly accused me.

I laughed. "No, that doesn't sound like me."

He smiled and nodded his head. "No, I'm pretty sure you definitely did," he argued, leaving no room to be persuaded otherwise. He stretched out his leg in front of him and bent one of his knees, dropping it to the side. "Gosh, I remember telling you everything up here," he said as his eyes examined every detail of his surroundings.

"Really?" I turned to him. I tried collecting my long lost memories and searched out the conversations we used to share here as kids.

"I could tell you anything. Any secrets we had, we knew they would be kept safe in here," he said as he looked over at me.

I adjusted my position and scooted a few inches away. Talking about secrets made me feel uneasy. Right now I had a pretty large one I was hiding. And after what had happened with Lane, I didn't feel like continuing to share it with others was a good idea. Not even Merritt.

"Remember when I was afraid of the woods?" he asked.

"I don't remember you being afraid of anything."

"Whenever we were out here playing, I found myself searching out into the darkness behind the trees. I remember the feeling of being followed and always thought there was someone out there. Just watching," Merritt explained.

He looked out the little wooden framed window and gazed off in the distance. The sunlight soaked in his skin and brightened his face as his dark eyes focused on the far off wilderness.

"One time I swear I saw someone. She was . . ."

"She?" I asked.

He went silent for a moment, then shook the idea from his head. "I don't know. It was so long ago. Now that I think about it, it was probably just a deer or something."

My mind flew back in time as I pictured the two of us playing in the fort as children. I imagined looking out the little window and seeing through the trees the hermit woman watching us from a distance.

I shivered.

So much time had passed since I met the witch and looked into the mirror. My old fears leaked out like a freshly opened wound. I tried to rationalize my thoughts to calm myself. I was never going to see her again. And I had no connection to anyone in the mirror like she said I would. The mirror was destroyed. The stranger from the reflection was nothing but a memory. As my brain fought to convince me of my safety, suspicion pressed against my instincts, like sensing a door left unlocked after leaving on vacation.

Without warning, the tree house made a loud crack and shifted to one side at least half a foot. The quick force of gravity caused Merritt to roll sideways, smacking his face into my shoulder. It caught us both unexpectedly, and I screamed.

"Okay, we need to go!" Merritt laughed and grabbed my hand as he started climbing out and descending down the ladder. I followed and crawled to the door behind him.

"Hurry," he chuckled as the tree house continued to moan and shake above us.

Before reaching the last step down, I lost my footing and started to slip. I twisted on the wobbly ladder, and my arm reached out grabbing Merritt's shoulder as he quickly caught me on the ground below.

I fell into his arms, and he held on as I regained my balance. A quick rush of his delicious scent flowed past my nostrils and triggered a shivering delight that poured down my ribcage. As we adjusted, we found ourselves meeting face to face. I held my breath as we stood for a moment awkwardly in each other's arms.

My muscles froze, and my mind went blank. I watched his twinkling eyes as he hesitated for a brief moment, glancing down at my lips then back into my eyes. My stomach began to tingle with bubbling warmth that hollowed my insides. After a second or two he finally stepped back to give me space to stand on my own.

Bending over, he swiped up my hat that had fallen off during the climb down and placed it lightly on top of his own head. The rugged cowboy look complemented his character and caused his already charming good looks to multiply ten times more.

"I'll walk you home," he said and began making his way back out in the direction of the dirt road.

Chapter 12

S o, for the final project you need to think big with me here," Shyler explained as she waved her pencil in the air in circles.

Reaching to her bedroom side table, she picked up her afternoon bowl of cereal. She had eaten almost every brown oat puff before touching any of the colorful marshmallows.

"That is so disgusting. You're about to eat an entire bowl of sugar," I said, staring at the soggy cereal.

"This is the best part of my snack and I worked hard on my self control to savor this little piece of marshmallow paradise. Life is too short to eat the gross bits and the yummies at the same time, Rylee."

As she swallowed a large spoonful, I looked away to avoid gagging.

"Okay, like I was saying," she said with her mouth full of milk. "Instead of a big speech for our class presentation, we have sock puppets . . ."

"Sock puppets?"

She swallowed. "Sock puppets teaching the class how to make tortilla bread."

I burst out laughing.

"No, seriously! I have it all planned out . . ."

There was a knock on Shyler's bedroom door.

"What is it, Mom?"

"I need your help for a second outside. Sorry to interrupt your studying," her mom apologized from the hallway. Shyler rolled her eyes as she threw her binder to the side and bounced off the bed.

"I'll be right back," she moaned and walked out her door. I laughed and looked back down at my textbook.

As the door closed behind her, Shyler's laptop on the nightstand made a twinkling sound, and I glanced up to see a message on the bottom corner of the screen. The note was accompanied by a chilling dark vulture icon.

"Hi, Rylee," it read.

I looked back to the door Shyler had just walked out of seconds before. Curious. Who knew I was at Shyler's house right now?

I shouted downstairs, "Shyler, are you typing from another computer?" No answer. I glanced out the window and saw Shy and her mom in the driveway unloading groceries from their car trunk.

Crawling over the bed, I scooted toward the computer. My fingers began typing across the keyboard.

"Who is this?"

I waited for a reply. Seconds later, I was greeted with another message.

"A secret admirer."

I laughed. Cute. I have a creepy stalker. Maybe someone was pulling some sort of prank. I made a list in my head of possible suspects.

"This better not be Lane!" I typed.

"Not Lane," they responded. I thought for a second.

"Merritt?" There was a pause.

"I don't know a Merritt yet. I'm just a devoted fan."

I was starting to get a little annoyed with my mysterious admirer and the lack of information I was receiving.

"Fan of what?" I pounded hard on the keys and waited. And waited.

"Your secret."

I sat back and pushed myself away from the screen as my breathing began to accelerate. Then I stood up and looked out the window again. Another message waited for me on the screen.

"We'll speak again soon."

Just then, Shyler walked back into the room.

"So, as I was saying about the puppets . . . Rylee, what's the matter?" She could see the look of shock in my pale, white skin.

"I . . . uh . . . nothing. I was just looking up puppet ideas." I quickly exited the message screen.

I couldn't sleep that night. I lay in the darkness trying to make out the shape of my spinning ceiling fan. As I watched it twirl, I attempted to lose myself in its continuous circular motion.

I needed to escape, and sleep seemed like the only way to close down my fast-paced, never-ending thoughts. They flickered through my head in disarray. It was as excruciating as trying to focus on the gaps between a speeding metro.

I began questioning who it was who could have messaged me earlier that afternoon. It wasn't Shyler. It wasn't Lane. Could one of them have told somebody? I trusted Shyler, and I don't think Lane would risk sounding insane. Maybe the woman in the woods had something to do with this. I shivered.

My back felt sore and stiff as I shifted from side to side. I attempted closing my eyes, but I couldn't stop them from opening almost immediately. I tossed and turned, frustrated.

The corner of my vision caught a beam of light that spilled out from under the doorway. I glanced at the clock on my desk.

Who else is awake this late?

Giving up on sleep, I walked out to discover the source of the mysterious brightness.

Down the hallway, Mom's painting room was lit up, and I could hear her shuffling around inside. My feet pressed against the coldness that emanated from the hardwood floor. Every step I took made a faint creak in the aching wood.

I leaned against the doorway and looked in the room. Mom sat silently, listening to the music in her headphones, and painting.

As she adjusted the corner of her canvas stand I noticed her wrists were looking thinner. Overall, she hadn't experienced many side effects from the cancer treatments, but it was becoming clear that she was losing weight. I closed my eyes to try and shut out the pain in my heart.

Perhaps there was a way I could help heal her with my gift. After all, if anyone deserved good karma, it would probably be safe to say my mother who birthed me and gave selflessly morning and night would be at the top of my list. The control over my power was strengthening more and more with each passing day, so I concentrated, confident I could save her if I pushed hard enough.

An unfamiliar sensation began to agitate my target. As I focused, the energy inside me became numb to my desires. I felt paralyzed and my power began slipping like beach sand between my fingers. There was something stopping me.

Mom pulled one bud out of her ear when she saw me and smiled.

"Hey," she whispered.

It wasn't working. Hiding my disappointment, I tried to return a cheerful smile. I walked through her maze piles of brushes and paints, sat down behind her, and watched, fascinated by her talented hands bringing enchanting colors to life.

The image she had created mesmerized me. It showed the scene of a man, young and handsome, lying in a grassy meadow near a pool of clear water. He was leaning over, peering down into the deep marsh.

"It's beautiful," I said. I watched as Mom began smudging a small figure's shadow behind a dark tree in the distance, spying on the man.

"What's with the creeper in the background?" I asked. She picked up a towel and patted her hands dry.

"That's Echo, the wood nymph. It's a love story. Well, I guess a one-way love story. It's kind of depressing," she explained. I looked closely at the shadow clutching the tree and could see her sadness, longing to be with the young man by the water. Just then, I noticed the man's charming reflection staring back up at him with great desire.

"Is this supposed to be Narcissus? Who fell in love with his own reflection?" I asked. Mom nodded and took off her glasses to clean off the splattered specks of grey paint.

"Echo once had been gifted with a lovely voice. The gods would come down just to hear her sing and tell stories. She captivated people with her words. So much so that she would distract Hera, the wife of Zeus, with her thrilling tales while he would go down and make love to the other nymphs," she explained.

I thought for a moment and laughed. "Wow. Zeus kind of sounds like a jerk."

Mom nodded her head. "Hera wasn't much better. She

decided to curse Echo for distracting her. Echo's voice was taken away, and she was only granted the ability to speak if she repeated what others had already spoken."

An echo. I thought of the times when I was younger visiting my cousins in the dry, desert canyon. We would take turns shouting at the top of our lungs and listening as our voices would bounce back and forth through the tall walls of red rock.

"She loved Narcissus. She would sit and echo him as he spoke words of deep adoration to his reflection. They both sat here waiting, wishing for the one they loved to return the affection, but neither one was ever granted their wish."

I gazed deeply into the picture and became lost in its emotions. I wanted to mourn with Echo because of her sorrows. No matter how long she called to him, Narcissus would never love her back. I furiously searched for the eyes in the shadow of the nymph and felt a sudden connection.

"Huh, you said she was cursed?" I asked.

"She could only mimic others," Mom replied.

I sat and thought. She could only mimic others based on what they said to her. I went back to bed. Moments later, I fell asleep.

I stood in a beautiful meadow. In the late, darkness of the night, the light of the stars lit the ground with glowing shades of pastel and azure. The sounds of chirping crickets and coquí frogs harmonized in sweet unison. I was surrounded by warmth and the continuous sparkle of colorful fireflies.

When I looked down, I found myself wearing a white, satin gown. The pure material wrapped tightly around my chest then draped down like a flowing toga.

My fingers stretched out and touched the tips of long

grass as I glided along a twisted path that led to a small fountain of water similar to the pool from the painting of Narcissus. A white light reflecting the ripples splashed against the vegetation surrounding the water.

My throat tightened and I thirsted for the pouring drink. As I leaned over to reach in, I became absorbed with the unexpected sight of the glowing reflection. It was my mother.

Her deep blue eyes had a silver haze in the lighting of the surrounding darkness. She was vibrant and youthful. It resembled a time when she was full of life and free from disease and I ached for this version of her to be a reality.

Past my mother's reflection, I could see deep in the water a small, flat figure buried beneath the floor of glossy pebbles. My heart gravitated toward it, and I began to reach into the pool, curious as to whether or not it was within my grasp.

A breath of wind rushed past me and whispered in my ear. I looked around to see if anyone was near. As I searched in the darkness, I saw the tree. I strained my eyes and tried to focus on the unfamiliar shapes. Behind the tree in the shadows, someone was there, watching me.

I woke up to the sound of Harrison downstairs banging on kitchen pots like a marching band percussion player. When I glanced at the clock I realized that I slept in much later than planned. My alarm must have gone off without my hearing it.

I ripped off the sheets and changed quickly, knowing I'd have to skip my morning shower. I grabbed a sweatshirt and reached for the nearest object to tie my hair back out of my face. All I could find was a red ribbon hanging from a shoebox full of crafts and art materials. Snatching my school bag and boots, I rushed down stairs.

The school day dragged on worse than ever before. I found myself glancing at the clock constantly. *Surely ten minutes have passed*, I'd think to myself, but each time I was utterly disappointed to discover that it had only been three minutes since I last checked the time. After painfully enduring what felt like eternity of lectures, school had almost come to an end for the day.

My phone fiddled in my hands as I watched the red hand slowly circle around the clock. I pulled up my contacts and searched for Merritt's number to text him. As I opened a blank screen to begin typing, I looked back up at the time and snapped my phone shut.

Merritt was the constant distraction of my thoughts, and I forced myself to hold back from communicating with him every waking minute of the day.

I needed to pace myself. Our last texting conversation happened when he woke me up yesterday to wish me a good morning. Surely thirty hours had been a long enough gap to text him again without feeling too clingy.

"Hey! Didn't see you at school today, ditcher! Where'd you go?" I finally typed.

My legs bounced up and down as I sat and waited impatiently for a response.

Then a reply, "I'm sick at home with the flu. I feel horrible."

Poor guy.

Once school was over, I ran to the market and picked out a mixture of comforting foods to create a thoughtful "get well" basket. After filling it with honey, soup, crackers, tissues, and lemons, I pulled my red bow from my hair and wrapped it around the gift for an extra special touch.

I left the market and sped to his house. The drive from town to our neighborhood seemed to take longer every time I traveled it.

Once I made it to his driveway, I tiptoed up to the porch to set the basket against the steps. The door suddenly swung open. Running late, Merritt's mother greeted me on her way outside.

Her short-cut highlighted hair fanned out at the sides, almost exactly like Merritt's. Her light caramel skin tone resulted from years of visits to the local tanning bed. She wore bright beaded jewelry that brought out the enchanting green in her eyes.

"Oh, honey, you are too sweet. He'll just love it! His room's right down the hall if you wanted to take it in to him yourself," she said, rushing to get to work.

I hesitated for a brief moment. "I would hate to intrude."

"Oh, nonsense!" she replied as she pushed me inside. She shut the front door behind her and left me alone in the big, quiet house.

The walls of the Emerson's home were composed of dark brown and black wood bands, giving the place a rustic cabin-like feel. Nothing was out of place, and the counters and shelves looked abnormally clean and polished. When his mother wasn't working, I imagined her spending her entire free-time cleaning.

I studied the family photographs as I made my way down the hallway. Portraits of Merritt, his older sister, and his mother hung staggered on the walls in black and white.

The hinges squeaked as I softly pushed his bedroom door open. When I walked inside, I immediately covered my mouth with one hand to hide my inching smile.

There was something adorable about how helpless Merritt looked, tangled in the covers and clutching his pillow like a childhood toy. The right side of his face was red with blanket lines from lying down, and his sleepy eyes squinted as they adjusted to the light in the room.

"Rylee?" He attempted to whisper through his hoarse voice.

"Oh my gosh. You look so miserable," I said, still trying to hide my smile. I set the basket of treats down on his nightstand and found a spot to sit beside him.

"Your mom just left. She said I could come in and drop this off for you."

He reached out from under the covers and grabbed my hand. "Will you keep me company for a while?"

He warmed my skin instantaneously. I reached up and felt his forehead. Heat radiated from his body like steam from a pot of boiling water. His fever must have been excruciating.

"I'd love to," I smiled.

He began to shiver.

"It's so cold in here."

He rolled over to his other side and pulled my arm in his direction. As he tugged me, I climbed in beside him and snuggled as closely as I could into the outline of his back. His shirt was damp from the sweat of his fever. Even now, he still had his delicious smell.

He moaned and squeezed my hand.

"Tell me something to distract the pain. My headache makes my brain want to jump out of my skull."

I laughed.

"Do you know the reason why we feel so miserable when we're sick?" I asked.

He closed his eyes and slowly shook his head. I leaned in closer and tucked my face between his neck and shoulder.

"I took a microbiology class last year. When a virus enters your immune system, your body's reaction is what causes the discomfort. Your fever right now is happening to kill the pathogens. There's a teeny, tiny battle taking place inside of you and you don't even realize it!"

I could tell by the frown on his face that my words weren't exactly comforting. He took a deep breath and gulped at the oxygen stuck in his throat.

"The best part is, once your immune system beats it, it learns and becomes stronger, so the next time it's invaded, it can kill the germs immediately. So, getting sick is good in a way. We grow because of it and become more protected."

"You're such a library nerd," he mumbled and smiled.

I laughed. "Yeah, I guess you're right. It really is fascinating though. And, if anything else, I guess sicknesses help us to be grateful. It makes you not want to take your health for granted. Right?"

I paused.

"Merritt?" I leaned over his shoulder to find him lightly snoring. I smiled and gently combed his thick hair out of his face with my fingers. Then quietly slipped out of the blankets and left, closing the front door behind me.

As I pulled out of his driveway and headed home, I began counting my blessings. I was thankful for my health. I thought of my sick mother but felt gratitude for her love and every second of happiness she brought to my existence. I was also grateful for Merritt and the fact that he was becoming a wonderful part of my life.

I walked into my home to the comforting aroma of baking butter and sweet sugar. Following the sound of laughter and music to the kitchen, I found Mom and Harrison smeared with flour and rolling cookie dough. The music player was sitting on the counter top turned up as they sang to Mom's old school classics and danced around the tiled floor.

I pulled out a stool beside the counter and stole a small

spoonful of dough from the mixing bowl. Harrison spread out his sticky fingers and unsuccessfully attempted to lick them clean without making a mess. The dough smeared against his cheek and on the tip of his hair and temples. Mom leaned over with a towel and cleaned his face, then kissed the side of his nose.

"Okay, little man. Time to change into pajamas," she said.

Harrison stood straight up in his chair. He exploded into the air and landed on his feet. Smiling, he made a loud screeching squeal as he ran as fast as he could like a race car to his bedroom upstairs. That child had a never-ending tank of bubbly energy.

As he left the music player shuffled and a slow love song unfolded into the air. Dad waltzed into the kitchen humming the pleasant new tune. He grabbed Mom around the waist and leaned over her shoulder to snatch a cookie she had delicately placed on the cooling rack.

"You little thief . . ." she scolded him as she turned to face him with her spatula raised.

"You don't know me," he teased and smoothly grabbed her side, spinning her to the beat of the soft music. She smiled and played along as he smoothly pulled the spatula from her fingers and sneaked it into his back pocket.

I watched them dance together as Dad tenderly pulled off Mom's glasses and lovingly kissed her face. They were a living fairy tale and I fell in love with the concept as I observed their quiet little romance. I pictured myself in the future, dancing and baking cookies with someone I cared for.

As my parents circled round and round, I soaked in their individual expressions. Each time their faces turned, I watched them stare in adoration at their soul mate.

It was a perfect moment until Mom started to

clutch Dad tightly and close her eyes in pain.

"Evelyn?" he asked, frightened.

"I'm sorry. I'm getting dizzy. I need to . . . I . . ." She trailed off. Her legs began to give out from under her. Dad caught all her weight so she could effortlessly slide to the ground. He knelt down gripping her shoulders as she held the sides of her head, waiting for the room to stop spinning.

"Mom?!" I shouted, my bar stool falling to the ground as I rushed to stand up. I felt cold and clammy as the warm rush of panic spread through my limbs.

Watching her collapse in exhaustion, my beating heart had clouded in a dark mist of terror. It felt like a stirring nightmare attacking my soul from every angle that I couldn't escape from. Although my emotions trembled violently on the inside, a chilling storm wrapped around me, freezing my body.

Dad pulled her in against his chest. He remained collected and his unflustered mood slowed the rush of anxiety filling the room.

I had to use every ounce of energy to pull on my retreating strength and break through the shock cementing my actions. I wrestled with it back and forth like a reeling battle between a fisherman and a monstrous sturgeon.

"Is there anything I can do to help?" I choked out between dry breaths, trying to cover the alarm that hailed inside of me.

I heard a faint sound behind me and looked back to see Harrison dressed in his striped cotton pajamas. He stood with eyes wide open as he watched Dad hold Mom in his arms.

I looked back at Dad, who nodded his head once, signaling me to go to Harrison. Spotting the cookies on the shelf, I grabbed a handful to distract him.

"C'mon Harris. Mom needs to rest for a while," I said as I led him back upstairs. I turned once more to look at Mom. She was staring back with a slight smile fighting to stretch across her face. Even in her moment of pain, she still managed to focus on my needs and comfort me with her cheerfulness.

I attempted again to use my power and heal her as she curled up in my father's arms, but once more I felt something block me. *Why am I broken?*

Harrison grabbed my hand and we silently climbed up the stairs. After brushing his teeth, he crawled into bed, and I tucked him in, looking into his dark, lost eyes.

"Mom is fine," I comforted. "She just got a little dizzy from dancing, that's all." I squeezed his tiny shoulder and smiled to hide the worry I felt inside. Reaching for his nightstand, I shut off the dully-lit desk lamp.

"She said you can't save her," Harrison whispered as I began to leave. My feet froze and I turned back to face him, puzzled by his remark.

"Harrison, what are you talking about? Mom told you this?"

His fingers lightly squeezed the bedspread below his chin. "An angel. An angel with white eyes."

A haunting ache gripped the inside of my stomach. No. The blind witch.

I fell down beside the bed to my brother's eye level and grabbed his arm. "Where did you see her, buddy? Where did you see this . . . angel? Did she hurt you?" My voice was shaking as I spoke.

Unlike the rattling emotions inside of me, his innocent face showed no concern or fear.

"I've seen her in my dreams. Sometimes she shows me things." He cupped his warm hand on my cheek. "Goodnight, sissy."

Harrison turned on his side and let out a soft exhale. Dread fell over me as I quietly left the room. Looking back, I watched the light of the hallway shining in around him slowly shrink smaller and smaller as the shadow of the closing door took its place.

I gripped the doorknob tightly and closed my eyes. I couldn't believe all of this was happening. Why did I ever choose to look in the black mirror? I wished I could take everything back and be normal once again. I never wanted to drag my family into this. Not little Harrison.

A giant weight of responsibility suddenly flooded over me. At that moment I made a promise to myself. No matter what happened, I would be there to protect my little brother.

I concentrated on grating the fear from inside of me. Forcing the heavy weight of air out of my lungs, I untied the stress that attempted to leach my emotions.

Timidly, I went back downstairs and saw a moving shadow under the door of my parents' room. I assumed Mom had regained her strength and was inside heading to bed.

In the kitchen I found Dad leaning against the sink, looking out the window into the black night. He shifted as he saw my moving reflection and tried to discreetly wipe the tears from his face before I could detect them. Then he turned to me and smiled.

"Mom's fine. She's turning in early for the night."

I had never seen my dad scared before. Ever since I was little, I had always admired his flawless courage. He was the fearless hero who smashed the monster spiders and shooed out the opossums from under the house with a plastic broom.

Reality gave me a hard blow as I realized he wasn't invincible. Mom's sickness was out of his control and wasn't something he could smash or shoo away with his bravery. Mom was slipping, and he could feel it.

I stood motionless as he walked over to me and wrapped his arms around me. His voice trembled as he reassured me that Mom was fine.

"She just needs to get some sleep," he explained. He let go and without looking at me, walked back to their room.

Standing all alone I stared at the cookies on the counter. I shook my head and began to distract myself by putting away the cookies, doing the dishes, and scrubbing any dirt on the counter I could find. After a half an hour, the entire kitchen was clean.

I shook my hands dry of the bubble suds and rested my forehead against the side handle of the refrigerator. The cool metal soothed the ache throbbing against my skull.

After a moment of enjoying the silence, I reached up to shut off the lights and climbed the stairs to my bedroom.

I curled into a tight ball and clasped my hands tightly around my stomach, trying to conceal the hollow feeling of worry inside my gut.

"I'm not afraid," I repeated, trying to convince myself. I shut my eyes tightly and begged my body to let me fade away, lost in sleep.

Chapter 13

The bite mark in my mouth had practically healed. I caught myself sucking the side of my cheek and thought about the night of the bonfire.

The curse must have backfired on me when Lane attacked. The wound in my mouth mimicked the pain of his bitten fingers. I began to piece together that the way I treated others naturally affected me too.

Then there was Mr. Kestler. I had gotten angry and gone overboard, allowing my power to destroy his vehicle. He didn't really deserve that. What if my action then in the coffee shop was what caused Mom to be sick last night?

All of my choices began to echo back into my life. I couldn't handle the idea of Mom experiencing pain because of the mistakes I had made. More guilt swelled inside me as I thought of little Harrison's nightmares and the part I played in those occurrences as well.

After school, the last place I wanted to be was at home. I felt like avoiding everyone was the best thing I could do for now and was what I needed. That afternoon I drove the car to the bottom of the town's hillside and parked near the water.

The river was calm and enchanting, a smooth sheet of

glass that stretched across the gorge and reached from the steamboat dock clear to the other shore.

I leaned against the railing and closed my eyes. Inhaling the fresh air, I soaked in the surrounding silence. My mind deflated and aired out everything that had happened around me.

I imagined the miraculous biblical stories of old and convinced myself that if I took one step off the dock, the river would catch me like a pillow foam pit, and I could walk across the mystical water and keep walking and never stop.

"Looks like a bad day for windsurfing."

A soft smile swept across my face at the recognition of Merritt's soothing voice.

"It's beautiful, isn't it?" I replied as he made his way toward me. His dark hoodie covered all but a small section of his hair swiped to the side above his eyes. He kept his hands warm in the front pockets of his jeans as he came closer.

"Yeah. It is beautiful," he agreed, smiling at me as he said it.

He stood by my side and looked out across the water. I felt a little cheerful knowing he was recovering from his sickness.

A moment passed, and I found my mind drifting away again. Merritt leaned in and studied my thoughtful expression.

"So, how's Rylee?" he asked. By his voice I could tell he sensed I was troubled.

"I don't know. Confused. Worried. Lost. I feel like I was given something that I am too weak to handle . . ." I stopped myself, realizing I had said too much. My curse was still a secret I had kept hidden from Merritt. But it felt good to tell him, even if he didn't understand what I meant by it. As the words flowed out, I began to feel more stable knowing he was listening.

"I just . . . I'm afraid of hurting everyone around me."

Merritt shifted his direction and looked thoughtful, as if trying to soak in my words.

I grabbed the railing in front of me, and right away Merritt's hand reached out and gripped mine. His movement was so sudden and unexpected. The contact sent a warm surge through my hand and up my arm, rushing through my entire body and settling in the pit of my stomach.

"You are strong, Rylee. You always have been. And whatever challenge you're experiencing right now, you'll make it through." He leaned in closer so our eyes were at the same level. "And I am here."

His last words made me want to collapse into his arms and let go of my fears. As badly as I hungered for his protection, I realized that I desired more and more to be there to protect him.

He smiled at me again.

"C'mon. There's somewhere I want you to see." He stretched his arm around my shoulder and pulled me away from the railing.

"The last time you said that, we ended up falling out of a tree."

"*We* didn't do anything. You're the one who fell out of the tree," he replied with a chuckle.

He gently steered me off the dock to the parking lot. Opening the passenger side door to his truck, he waited for me to climb inside.

"Where are we going?" I sat staring out the window as the Ponderosa pine trees flashed by in a huge blur of forest green.

"It seems to me like you need a break from everything. So, we're going out and adventuring. Like the good old days."

I had a flash of a childhood memory of Merritt wearing his red bandana hanging by the branch of an old willow tree. "Grab ahold, lass!" he had yelled as he reached for my hand to pull me up to his high watchtower. My little, yellow dress made of shiny tulle and ribbons snagged on a piece of bark as he lifted me. I grabbed his shoulder to stabilize myself. With gentle hands, he pushed my golden tiara out of my eyes and whispered in my ear, "You're safe with me, your highness."

The truck parked in a little nook of trees just off the main highway. I hesitated before unbuckling my seatbelt, trying to determine where we had stopped.

"Is it okay if your shoes get a little wet? Because we'll probably be trudging through some water," Merritt said as he climbed out of the car.

"Whoa, whoa, whoa! Wait a second! You never said ANYTHING about getting wet. That's ice-cold, freshly melted snow water!" He ignored my complaining and grabbed his jacket out of the bed of the truck.

"It won't be that bad," he lied. "And it'll be worth it. I promise." He tossed me his jacket and began walking toward the trees. As I adjusted my arms into the sleeves, I pressed the collar against my face and inhaled his comforting scent.

He led me down a faded trail to a clear, pebbled stream bordered with tall walls of natural rock formations. The water slid over the rocks like icing on a freshly frosted cake. Merritt beckoned me to follow as he began trekking through the creek.

"There's no land trail. We have to walk through the stream to get there," he informed me as I stood stubbornly on the dry ground. Realizing he would be leaving with or without me, I reluctantly joined him in the water.

It was bitter cold. The temperature stung my ankles like a thousand needles. It was the same type of horrible pain I felt in my skull after drinking smoothies too fast. With every step I took I concentrated on not letting Merritt see my misery. I shut my mouth tightly to keep my teeth from chattering. Whenever he would look over his shoulder to check on me, I faked a smile.

Yet, even with the freezing water, I couldn't help but stare at the beautiful scenery. The bright green trees clung to the colossal stone walls. As we crawled over fallen tree trunks and ducked through the wild vines overhead, I truly appreciated the nature that surrounded me for the first time.

When my parents were younger they had moved across the country and my mother explained how she had never been aware of the beauty of the northwest until it was taken from her. The Washington wilderness healed her homesickness as soon as they moved back, and she knew then that it would always be her permanent home.

"Here it is!" Merritt shouted from up ahead, waiting for me to catch up. When I turned the corner I was sprayed with the cool mist from a giant waterfall. The white water tumbled down and broke apart into tiny droplets as it fell from the tip of the hill to the stream below.

With an inviting hand, Merritt reached out and guided me around the falling torrent to a small opening that led us into a cave-like nook behind the falls. We rested on the wet stone and watched from the inside as the water foamed and poured down in front of us.

The sound of the crashing water rushed into my soul, cleansing it of all the toxins that I felt were polluting me. This place was exactly what I needed. It was the perfect escape.

I leaned over to Merritt and whispered, "Thank you. It's beautiful."

When I looked up our eyes met. Perhaps it was from the shadows of the cave, but I noticed he looked at me in a new way—almost as if he wanted to tell me something but didn't know how to translate it into words. And maybe I was caught in the magic of the cave as well, because my heart suddenly stirred.

I had something he needed to know too. I wanted this moment, just the two of us here, to last forever.

I forced myself to pull my eyes away and stood up. I realized I was standing so close to the innards of the waterfall that I could reach out and touch it with my hand.

The breeze blew my hair back, and the glow of the mist sparkled around me. The white noise of falling water splashed in my eardrums almost like a comforting whisper. It whispered for me to tell him . . . Tell him what he meant to me.

My throat went dry as I tried to swallow. I couldn't allow my fear to cloud my actions. A burst of courage flew me through the wave of worry, and I was ready. I quickly spun around.

"Merritt!"

With the distraction of the whispering water, I hadn't noticed that he had stood up right behind me. He was right there, our bodies almost touching. Before I could let out the words, he gently caressed my face and pushed his lips against mine.

I couldn't breathe. I had forgotten how. My fingers instinctively reached up and ran through his thick, dark hair. He slightly pulled back his face and smiled, causing our noses to tangle together.

If I hadn't already felt like I was dreaming, I would have wished never, ever to wake up now. We enveloped ourselves in each other's arms as his soft lips brushed against my cheek. I closed my eyes, lost in his sweet scent. His chest was warm and welcoming, and his protective arms shielded me from the drizzling moisture of the waterfall.

Whatever it was that we both needed to confess earlier was already spoken through that single kiss.

Leaning back, my sneaker slipped on the slick rocks. I screamed out and my reflexes caused me to grip Merritt's neck tightly. We both lost our balance and fell back through the dropping water into the shallow pool outside the cave. The stunning cold pumped my already flowing adrenaline and awakened all of my senses.

Merritt quickly popped above the water and shook his head, causing his soaked hair to plaster against the side of his forehead. The icy temperature altered his skin tone, and the freckles that covered his nose and cheeks stood out like the brown flecks on a robin's egg.

In the water we both started laughing through our violent shivers. I floated to the side and Merritt followed quickly behind.

He reached for me through the water and pulled me back in close. My teeth began to chatter in rhythm as I gazed once more into those enchanting eyes. His features were too irresistible and I sprang up to kiss him again.

My shivering came to a halt as his distracting touch numbed the coldness surrounding me. Droplets of water rushed down our faces and caught in the cracks of our warm lips. I pressed my hands against his solid stomach, soaking in all of his warmth. He let go, and I opened my eyes.

My visual focus began to expand. Behind him I noticed an unusual ripple gliding along the top of the water. A thin, black sliver broke the surface and moved directly toward us. It took just a moment to process before realizing what it was.

"Water snake!" I shouted. With great speed, Merritt jerked to the side and jumped back. I had never seen a human move so fast.

"I HATE SNAKES!" he screamed and leaped through the water, kicking up and hurdling over the current like an Olympic athlete.

I tried to run, but my foot slipped again underneath me.

By the time Merritt looked back and realized I wasn't with him, he quickly turned and yelled at himself, "Wait! What am I doing? Hold on, I'm coming!"

I burst into laughter. The entire situation was hilarious. He looked ridiculous running back and forth. And more outstanding was that I had just witnessed him shrivel in fear over a tiny snake.

The cold temperature of the water drained all my coordination, and I fell over and over again, trying to catch my balance and move on the wet rocks.

Merritt grabbed me and effortlessly threw me over his shoulders. He continued to high-knee his way out of the water as he mumbled under his breath about how much he despised snakes.

By the time we reached land my stomach muscles were aching from laughter. We both lied flat on our backs on the shore, trying to catch our breath.

"You—were—so—brave," I tried to let out between chuckles.

"This moment," he attempted to say in a serious tone, "stays between you and me."

After we quit laughing and our abs recovered from the ache, he reached out and held my hand. Even the simple touch of his fingertips on mine gave me instantaneous butterflies. We stayed there, soaking up the sun, until the day passed without us realizing it.

"I should probably get back," I said, disappointed. We began to head back up the trail, and I stopped in my tracks, turning to him.

"Thanks, Merritt. Today was perfect."

He leaned in and kissed me once more. I couldn't remember the last time I had felt this happy.

My ruffled gray bedspread was covered in textbooks, homework, and unfolded laundry. I switched on my music and sat cross-legged against the headboard to begin folding my socks into piles of unmatched pairs.

As the songs played in the background, I quietly harmonized to the melodies. I really did love to sing but never enough to let those around me listen too closely.

As I tidied up and organized the bed, I could hear the tinkling sound of my phone ringing faintly inside the crease of my pillowcase. Shyler's name lit up in bold letters across the screen.

"Hi, Shy," I answered and stretched out my legs over the piles of clothes.

"Hi, ma'am. It's nice to know you're alive and haven't been thrown into some ditch to die somewhere."

Sensing the slight irritation in her voice, I realized I hadn't been able to give her much of my attention lately. I felt a small pang of guilt for my lack of contribution to our friendship. Neither of us ever brought up what happened with Lane the night of his party. I knew she didn't blame me, but it still must have crushed her, knowing she had held feelings for him.

"Yeah, I've been a bit busy lately."

"Hanging out with Merritt. Yes, the world knows and

is incredibly jealous. You have to tell me everything. Has he kissed you yet?"

I paused and bit my lip.

"You're not answering, Rylee!"

I fiddled with my hair and could feel my cheeks beginning to blush. I attempted to change the subject.

"So, how is your studying coming along for our big kiss—QUIZ! . . . quiz coming up?" Change of subject plan: Failed.

"You totally did! Why didn't you tell me?" she squealed. "I'm so excited! This is fantastic news! Wait, what else happened? Rylee, it was only a kiss, right?"

Well, I supposed she would have found out eventually. And it was refreshing to hear her cheerful self again knowing she had speedily forgiven me for the lack of attention she'd been receiving.

She began to rattle off: "Remember who you are! Choose the right! Protect your virtue!"

"Oh my gosh, Shyler. You're such a Mormon," I interrupted. "I have to go. I'll talk to you about it tomorrow." I hung up the phone and tossed it across the bed.

As I began to gather my spinning thoughts, a foam dart launched through the crack of my doorway and hit me square in the nose. From outside my room, Harrison giggled and shuffled away downstairs.

"Okay."

I threw down the folded socks and bolted out of my bedroom. Catching up to him by the bottom step, I lifted him upside down and carried him to the kitchen, tickling his sides. He squirmed and cried out with absolute delight.

"Careful, you two," Mom lightly cautioned as we circled and stumbled through her cooking space. I set

Harrison down and threw a dish towel over his head as he scurried away.

"Can I help with anything?" I asked as Mom stirred spaghetti sauce over the stovetop. The smell of fresh tomatoes and basil warmed my senses. Before letting her answer, I began setting out plates and silverware.

I turned and glanced out the window. Out of the corner of my eye a dark shadow caught my attention.

"Oh, gosh!"

To my absolute horror, I saw the old hermit woman, staring straight back at me. Her smoky eyes glistened and struck me with fear. Feeling dizzy, I grabbed the table for support.

"Rylee! Are you okay?"

I looked down and concentrated on my feet while I tried to catch my breath. When I looked back outside, she was gone.

"Ry, what's wrong?" Mom asked, concerned.

I tried to control my panicking breaths and to calm my nerves.

"Uh, I'm fine. Just a muscle cramp," I lied. I glanced outside once more, haunted by the emptiness where the blind witch had stood just moments before.

Chapter 14

The coffee shop was slow and lonely. Mr. K hadn't come back to order his regular lattes since the car incident. Near closing hours hardly anyone stopped by for coffee anyway.

To kill time I began sweeping around the restaurant under the chairs and tables. I paused for a second to adjust my black apron and scanned the almost empty room.

Seated at the corner of the bar was an elderly man slowly stirring his black coffee. I could see the dirt underneath his fingernails as he set his spoon neatly on his paper napkin. His gray beard billowed down his chest when he looked down at his drink. He wore an antique leather hat with ear straps that folded up over the sides and brown, pointy cowboy boots under his lightly faded jeans.

He sat silently and drank his cup, keeping to himself. He was kind and gentle and hardly spoke a word unless spoken to. Something about his silence made him mysterious and made you long to know the secrets hidden behind his eyes.

Secrets. I'd grown to hate that word.

I turned around to the sound of the jingling bell hanging against the door handle and smiled as Merritt's familiar face entered the room.

"Hey! You said you wanted to meet me?" he greeted.

"Is it 5:30 already? I just have to clock out real quick." I grabbed the broom and dustpan and ran to the back to hang up my work clothes.

My hands began to sweat and my stomach churned as I realized what I was planning to do. After all the recent events, I decided that I needed to be honest with Merritt and finally tell him about my gift.

I trusted him; I was just nervous that it would freak him out. Fear tickled inside me that this would be too much for him. *What if he doesn't believe me? He might think I'm crazy. What if he DOES believe me?*

I sneaked back behind the coffee counter next to the other barista counting out the register and made two smoothies before meeting Merritt outside.

He was sitting in a large brick window of the building next door. He scooted over to make room and I handed him one of the drinks as I sat down beside him.

"So, what's our meeting about today, Miss Perry?"

I tried to hide my seriousness and somehow managed to fake a smile, even though I was terrified inside. I thought long and hard about my choice of words and put everything as delicately as possible.

"You know our tree house, how we can trust each other with any secret?" I began.

He nodded his head.

"Well, since it's falling apart and probably too dangerous to climb in, can we dedicate this window nook as our new treasure chest of safely kept secrets?"

He reached up his finger and crossed his heart.

The sweat on my hands was almost dripping, and my stomach began to feel nauseated. I struggled to form the words and to allow them to escape my tongue.

"I . . . I . . . have something . . . There is something

about me that no one else is capable of."

Merritt's expression didn't change. He just sat back and soaked in my words. To escape my uneasiness, I focused on my fingertips, brushing away the dust that rested in the cracks of the old, red bricks.

"I have a gift . . . or a curse . . . call it whatever you want."

I could feel my neck turning red, but as I looked back over at Merritt, he still continued to act natural. My concentration shifted to control the deep, shaky breaths that weakly traveled through my lungs.

"I have the ability to control a person's luck. Depending on how they treat me, they can immediately receive a natural consequence. It's not ME that rewards them or punishes them, but THROUGH me, life creates immediate justice for their actions, like an echo."

He still maintained composure. *He hasn't started freaking out yet. What's happening?*

"So if someone tries to hurt me, they end up getting hurt. And the opposite of that . . . That's why Lane was trying to . . . well . . ." I trailed off.

His eyes shot up at me, but even now, he remained levelheaded. I was stirring inside. My mind clawed at his expression in desperation to know what he was thinking. *Why is he so calm?* It was almost driving me crazy.

"Merritt, why aren't you freaking out right now?!"

He looked at me and smiled. Placing his hand on the back of my head, he leaned in so our foreheads were touching.

"I think I always knew somehow that there was something peculiar about you. I guess I had already accepted that a while ago."

I could tell he was pausing to review his words in his mind before speaking, making sure his expressions were absolutely clear.

"Rylee, when I kiss you, my entire universe freezes, and I feel like I'm being kissed back 100 times more. I care for you so deeply, and that emotion pours back into me from you so intensely, like being hit by a semi."

I sat flabbergasted, bathing in his words.

"And I am always happy. When I'm around you, that happiness feels like some sort of high. It's not normal. I knew then you were no ordinary girl. Not just like a crazy, uncontrollable crush, like . . . scientifically there had to be an explanation for why you made me feel this way. What you're saying makes total sense to me."

I just stared at him. How? How was this person sitting in front of me so capable of remaining perfectly composed after what I had just told him? Why was he not surprised? When had he figured this out before?

"Wow," I said. "I was NOT expecting that reaction from you, that's . . . that's just . . ." I couldn't find the words. I was completely in shock by his immediate acceptance of who I was. Merritt truly was amazing.

He sucked the last bit of smoothie from his cup as it made a loud gargling noise.

"What flavor did you get?" he asked, setting his cup on the ground.

That was it.

My deep, dark secret was officially accepted. Nothing had changed in our relationship, except the topic of conversation.

"Pumpkin pie."

I held it out for him to try. He grabbed it and took a tiny sip, then tilted his head to the side and paused, trying to decide if he liked it.

"This is disgusting," he said. He quickly pulled off the lid and tipped my cup upside-down, splattering orange smoothie everywhere on the sidewalk.

"What are you doing?!"

He chuckled. "I'm sorry. I've always wanted to do that." He laughed so hard a tear began to form in the corner of his eye, and he reached up with his thumb to wipe it away.

"You jerk!" I laughed as I pushed him away from me. Merritt Emerson, always full of surprises. He stood up and began walking back inside.

"I'll go buy you a new one. I'm sorry. You should have seen your face!" He kept laughing.

I couldn't help but giggle to myself as I brushed off drops of pumpkin that had splashed onto my shoes.

When Merritt opened the door to walk inside, his heel slipped on a small, melted puddle of cream. He staggered to the side to catch his balance. The remaining trickle of smoothie leaked out of the cup and down the side of his pants. He looked down at the mess and silently nodded.

"Yes, this would make sense," he muttered to himself.

"Immediate justice," I replied in satisfaction.

A long, playful sigh escaped through the edges of his mouth. He turned and continued making his way inside the shop.

I reviewed in my mind our conversation that had just taken place about my secret. I leaned my head back against the window and smiled. I had nothing to be afraid of. He still cared for me and knowing about my curse didn't change a thing.

Merritt returned with another smoothie and two scones in his hand. His lips stiffened as he tried not to smile. He leaned over and handed me the drink and a scone and kissed the top of my head.

"I'm sorry," he said. Nestling back into his spot in the window, he reached up and put an arm around my shoulder hugging me. Smiling to himself, he took a bite of scone. "I always knew you were special, Rylee."

Merritt came home with me after we finished our drinks and scones. We sat on the porch swing wrapped in a warm blanket and reminisced about the hot summers of the past.

Merritt's fingers brushed through my hair as I rested my head against his chest, listening to his steady heartbeat.

When I thought about it, I was amazed with his heart's consistent pulse. No matter what happened in the world around us, peace and wars, health and sickness, as we mourned and danced, wept and laughed, our hearts just kept pumping, secured in their bordered ribcages of tissue beating on and on through every moment. Life was simple. The heart had one assignment and performed it beautifully.

I took a deep breath and held Merritt tighter. How grateful I was for his heart. It was the reason he existed, and its constant beat allowed him to be here and a part of my life.

Around the corner of the house, Beck came dashing out with a feathered headband falling off the side of her furry ears. Closely behind her, Harrison followed with a plastic ax, covered in red and yellow stripes of face paint and screaming in his high falsetto.

"Harrison, leave that poor dog alone!" I laughed. He tumbled over onto his stomach. The tall, green grass in the yard covered his tiny bare chest.

He eyed Merritt solemnly, trying to determine if this new face was friend or foe. Merritt smiled and playfully stuck out his tongue. A huge grin slid across my brother's face as he rolled up out of the grass and joined us on the porch.

"Hey, buddy, this is Merritt. Would you like to say 'hi'?" I asked, already knowing the answer.

Harrison was extremely timid around people he didn't know. The fact that he had approached me on the porch with someone unfamiliar nearby was a surprise in and of itself. I hardly expected him to say anything.

He silently grabbed my hand and began pulling me up out of the swing to follow him. Merritt and I exchanged glances, deciding a little walk would do us good.

As we trailed behind Harrison and Beck to the woods, Merritt reached down and grabbed my hand. His thumb brushed back and forth against my skin, and I took a step closer, allowing our arms to tangle together. My empty hand reached up and cupped his upper arm.

Along the path of the nearby stream Harrison stopped at a tiny beaver pond inlet and watched the water skippers glide along the surface.

I sat in a small sandy patch of ground next to Beck, who moaned and slowly rolled onto her back beside me. I scratched her stomach and enjoyed the quiet of the nearby flowing water.

Merritt stood over by Harrison, kicking the rocks and pebbles beside the pond. My brother giggled as he tried to catch the water bugs and kept looking up at Merritt to make sure he was noticing and equally amused.

He seemed to find Merritt just as curious as I did and enjoyed every second of his attention. After a few minutes of catching skippers and tadpoles, Harrison turned to Merritt and said in a soft voice, "My mom's dying."

My mouth dropped in shock. I had never imagined that my sweet brother had picked up on the seriousness of the situation with my mother. At that age I had never been aware of anything except for myself. It killed me knowing that I hadn't been able to protect him from what was happening around him. I wanted to hold Harrison in my arms, to turn against the line of fire and use myself as a human shield to block his heart from all of the pain.

Silently, Merritt squatted down so he was level with

Harrison. A wrinkle formed between his eyebrows as he focused on my brother's innocent face. In his eyes I could see concern, love, and understanding. It was the same way he looked at me when he listened.

"I think one of my last memories I have of my dad before he died was when I was about your age," he said.

As he spoke, I realized I had never asked Merritt about his father. All I knew was that he was absent. I assumed perhaps that his parents were separated or that his dad had abandoned them when he was younger. My heart ached knowing Merritt had suffered through the loss of his father as a child.

"My dad and I were out at the lake, and he taught me a trick. Will you let me teach you?" Merritt asked. Harrison nodded his head. Smiling, Merritt ruffled his bright, bowl-cut hair. He reached down and picked out a smooth, flat rock. I watched as he positioned it in Harrison's hand and taught him how to flick it so it skipped across the still water.

After a few failed attempts, Harrison was able to get it to skip twice on his own. Merritt stood up and quickly flung his own rock. We all watched as it bounced six times across the clear pond.

"Wow!" Harrison exclaimed and began gathering as many smooth rocks as he could find.

I stared in adoration at Merritt as he glanced back in my direction. Besides my mother, I had never met another human being as sweet and genuine as he was.

I quietly mouthed, "Thank you." He knew exactly how to cheer up my little brother.

Merritt grinned back and began helping Harrison collect more skipping stones.

Chapter 15

All day long, I thought about Merritt. Into the night, while I drifted to sleep, he crowded the focal point of my mind.

When I took in a deep fresh breath of air, his face dissolved from my view, and I found myself standing on an old, paved road. The rolling hills in the distance touched the shadows of color of the dusky sky. Sherbet orange soaked into pinks and violets that faded above me into the darkness of the night. The bordering lights of the recently set sun scraped at the night sky with its outstretched fingers before slipping away and fading into nothing.

I was lost in this unknown valley and searched desperately for familiar landmarks to guide me. Up above, the bright moon beamed down on the pathway in swirls of blues, greens, and grays encompassing the surface.

My eyes caught the familiar shape of a person walking toward me. I waited and suddenly recognized the face of the hermit from the woods. Her tiny, distant figure slowly crept in closer.

As she made her way, I caught myself gazing up again into the night sky and stood captured in the glimmering half-sphere. The glowing light felt different than the moon I had always known. I felt an intimate connection pulling me toward it and toward the twinkling stars that grew brighter and brighter as the night continued taking over the sky.

My eyes dropped back down to the hermit standing directly in front of me.

"He is coming for you, balancer," she whispered. In her misty eyes' reflection, I could see my own colorless expression glazed with panic.

"Who's coming for me?"

"The one tied to the connection of the black mirror. He has seen what you are capable of. He desires what you have and will not stop until you are in his possession."

An admirer of my power. He must be the one who messaged me from Shyler's computer that day. What does he want with my gift?

The witch reached up toward my face and again, pressed her icy cold fingers against my eyes. I could feel her trying to show me something. A face flashed into my mind, and I could see the crisp details of the stranger as clearly as if he were standing right in front of me.

The man had a younger looking face with a smooth, hairless head. His piercing, narrow eyes were a vibrant shade of light blue. With flawless skin, his face seemed long with an acutely angled chin.

He towered over me in height and wore a dark jacket and slacks. One thing that stood out to me was his older generation, leather shoes.

The witch pulled her hands from my face and the man disappeared from my sight.

"Remember," she cautioned. "You are not the only one with special gifts."

I glanced once more at the unfamiliar sky.

"HE'S COMING!" she shrieked.

I shot up out of bed in panic, gasping for air and felt the coolness of the cracked window in my bedroom as the covers fell from my bare shoulders. My eyes searched the dark, familiar room. I pushed my tangled hair out of my face, and my heart began to steady as I realized it was only a dream.

Although my feelings of anxiety deflated from the inside of my chest, there was a faint warning in my heart that more changes in my life were swiftly approaching.

A ringing sound from my computer suddenly caught my attention. I stumbled over and tried to translate the blurry message on the screen with my drowsy eyes.

"Hello again, Rylee."

I recognized the mysterious sender who had chatted with me at Shyler's house the day we were studying. The eerie photo of the dark vulture greeted me with bitterness.

I rubbed my puffy eyelids to clear my vision.

"Mr. Secret Admirer, I don't have time for this. I need to sleep," I typed.

A message appeared again, "She warned you about me, didn't she?"

All my weariness vanished immediately and was replaced with fear churning in the pit of my stomach. I peered between the dusty blinds out the window then quickly snapped them shut, closing out the darkness behind the glass.

I reflected on the memory of the blind witch from my recent dream picturing the narrow faced man with bright blue eyes she had shown me. The long sleeves of his old coat were somewhere in the darkness, skimming across a keyboard as he messaged me and played games with my head.

My fingers hesitated between each word, "Who are you?"

I waited as moments passed by before I saw any response. My arms began to shiver from the chilling air surrounding me.

"I know about your gift, Rylee. I want to help you."

Help me? I pondered his statement while reaching for the cotton shirt that rested behind my chair. Pulling it up over my head, I slid it on halfway to combat against the coldness.

"How?" I typed.

"I can teach you how to become stronger, how to perfect your gift. We need to meet somewhere . . . *alone.*"

What?! Is this a joke? Yeah, I'll go ahead and run off to who knows where with a sketchy stranger that somehow has access to stalking and invading my privacy. Whatever tricks this man was playing, they needed to end now.

I quickly responded. "It's just that I was told this thing once when I was like two years old not to trust strangers. So, I'm gonna go ahead and pass on the offer. And I would appreciate you no longer contacting me." The confidence in my reply was to try and cover the anxiety inside me. I was worried about my safety. If it was this easy for him to find a way to communicate with me, surely knowing where I lived wouldn't be a challenge either. That is assuming he didn't know already.

"Rylee, I don't want you to regret this. Keep in mind that eventually you WILL change your mind. I'm very persuasive. If you choose to come with me now, no one will be harmed."

I started to tremble. I began taking short breaths and held the sides of the desk for balance.

"Are you afraid, Rylee?"

I looked at his message and tried to contain my emotions. I pressed my lips together and sucked in air through my nose. As I thought about his words, my fear turned to anger. I did have a gift, and I would use it to protect myself. My fingers attacked the keyboard.

"You can't hurt me without hurting yourself! If you think I am afraid, then you should be terrified. No matter what you try and do to me, I'll take that pain and unleash it right back. You can't touch me."

After sending the message, I shut off my computer. I had had enough of these games. Whatever this dangerous man had planned for me, I convinced myself I would be stronger, and if it was a continuous battle to see who could endure the pain the longest, I promised myself that I would be the last one standing.

Chapter 16

The obnoxious buzz of my persistent alarm clock hammered at my brain as I hid under the covers and blindly felt around for the snooze button on the nightstand. Frustratingly, I pushed every button on the clock as the noise continued. As a last resort, I shoved it off the desk. The alarm silenced as it slammed to the ground.

The comfort of the heated blankets warmed my curled up body from head to toe. I let out a silent whimper as I slowly crept out of my cozy cocoon into the chilling air hovering above my covers.

Bright blue beams of early morning light crept through my window and glossed the room. My yawning and stretching began to awaken my senses as I made my way downstairs.

I walked in the kitchen to find Mom dressed for the day. She sat at the table reading her tablet. Next to her lay a pile of handwritten papers and a plate of half eaten wheat toast.

"How are you feeling?" I asked as I opened the fridge to grab a carton of orange juice.

"Stellar," she replied and continued reading and writing.

Beck moaned and waddled over to my feet from under the table. Her white-tipped tail swayed back and forth as she waited by the door to be let outside. I could tell by her round belly and noticeable weight gain that Harrison had mastered his stealth mode ability to sneak unwanted dinner scraps under the table.

After letting her out, I walked behind Mom and peered over her shoulder.

"Whatcha working on?"

"I'm making a bucket list."

I began to read the first three lines:

1. Finish my paintings
2. Watch the sunset at the beach
3. Take Rylee wedding dress shopping

"Wedding dress shopping?!" I laughed. "Isn't that an automatic given? I'm sure when I'm old enough to get married I'll be nice enough to ask my mom to come shopping with me. I thought bucket lists were supposed to be dreams to complete before . . ." I cut myself short and couldn't complete my sentence, realizing what I was about to say: *before you die.*

Mom looked down at her hands and sat in silence for a second then switched off her tablet and smiled.

"I just wanted to make sure I had all my important dreams checked off."

My stomach dropped. I felt horrible for what I had said. Mom was scared that she wouldn't live long enough to be there for the simple little moments, and I stood there mocking her dreams. I tried to think of what I could say to cheer her up again.

"Well, I guess a person doesn't technically have to be engaged to try on wedding dresses. Or have a boyfriend. Or even have a boy interested in her before she can shop for her dress, right? Just for fun?"

Her eyes lit up, and she scooted back out of her seat.

"How important are your classes today? Do you have any big tests, or can you make up the work easily?"

She reached for her cell phone.

"There shouldn't be anything huge happening. I can get most of the homework assignments from Shyler. Why?" I asked puzzled.

Mom punched in a phone number and listened while the other line rang.

"Hi, yes, this is Evelyn Perry, Rylee's mother. I just wanted to call and let you know she won't be making it to school today." She smiled at me and began tracing a quick doodle of a wedding dress in the corner of the paper next to her hand.

I smiled. Forgetting all about my orange juice, I hurried back upstairs and began to shower to get ready for our adventure-packed day of playing hooky.

The dress shop in town had the taste of charm mixed with a tiny drop of shabby. Its glass windows greeted us with glamorous dresses, each begging to be taken home and adored.

We walked into the quiet shop as a sales associate lady in her mid-thirties greeted us by the door. Her short, stout body frame reminded me of a small, round teapot.

"Shopping for wedding dresses, ladies?" she asked as she finished organizing a nearby shelf of flower girl tutus.

Mom and I exchanged glances and nodded.

"Well, congratulations, when is the big day?" she asked excitedly, turning in my direction.

"Um," I looked back at Mom and panicked. "I'm not actually engaged."

The lady nodded her head without any look of judgment.

"Oh, those boys sure know how to take their sweet time popping the question, don't they?" She laughed hysterically, tossing her head from side to side to catch our eyes. Her intense laughter caught us both off guard and almost made me jump.

Mom gave a courteous laugh to ease the awkwardness. Cheerfully, the lady bounced to the back to prepare a dressing room.

Once she was out of sight I stared at my mom with eyes wide open.

"Well, she is just friendly, isn't she?"

Mom covered her mouth with her hand to silently hold back her giggling.

The woman came back with an armful of dresses and herded me into the backroom like an energetic sheepdog scurrying from side to side.

As I began to undress, one of the gowns caught my attention on the hanging rack. I singled it out and studied the glimmering jewel design that covered the entire top half of the dress, then trickled down into spiral sections of the long skirt.

It amazed me how something as simple as a blanket of material could reach out, like it had a soul or a personality. The dress smiled at me and whispered expressions of persuasion to try it on.

"Oh, you would look darling in this one," the lady spoke behind me as she watched me eye the gown. "I'll help you put it on. I won't bite," and again let out her thunderous laugh.

Lifting the white material over my shoulders, she helped fluff it out and zipped me up in back.

The sleeveless top fit comfortably around my chest like it was designed and sewn just for my unique size. The shiny bottom spread out and bunched up in billowing ruffles, giving it a frosted cupcake look.

"Beautiful," she said, and escorted me out to show my mom sitting patiently on the side couches. The skirt crunched and swished with every delicate step. I stood on my tiptoes to avoid getting the edges dirty as it glided across the carpet.

My mom stood up and gasped, "Oh, my." She clasped her hands and held them against her lips. "You look absolutely stunning."

"Thanks, Mom." I knew she had to say that. As I rolled my eyes, her words made me faintly blush.

I was led to a raised stool that stood in front of a wide-angled mirror. The beauty of the dress in the reflection managed to catch me off guard. Compared to how I saw it draped on the hanger, wearing it now made it completely come to life and look even better than I had expected. I had no idea a dress could make a person shine in such an elegant, tasteful way.

"That's not even the best part," the dresser lady said as she hit a light switch, turning off the bright lamp above my head. As I stood in the darkness, she reached for a separate switch and slowly twisted the light knob.

Below my feet, small white lights gradually faded on, causing the beaded jewels of the dress to sparkle in purples and silvers. The beads of light glittered in every direction of the room, almost like a diamond.

"Wow." The word slipped out of my own mouth without me realizing it.

My mother turned her profile to the side to try to wipe away a tear without anyone noticing. The teapot lady put one arm over her shoulder and loudly announced, "Don't worry, honey. This is the part where all the moms cry."

We all adored the glimmering gown for another moment before I ran back to change. I looked longingly at the dress one last time, then set it on the rack and tried shaking the thought of weddings from my head.

A new Thai Restaurant had recently opened in town, and Merritt and I couldn't wait to try it. We drove in for a quick lunch between classes. Merritt sat with his elbow on the table holding up his chin, staring off with a look of deep concentration.

"So, how's Merritt?" I asked, interrupting his train of thought. His eyes shifted to me and his expression transitioned, adding a splash of curiosity.

Dropping his elbow, he leaned back in his chair and asked, "Will you tell me what the deal is with girls and weddings?"

My fork slipped out of my hands. Trying to act quickly, I began bending over to reach it and hit my forehead on the table. *Oh, gosh.*

"Weddings? I, uh, don't . . . What do you mean?"

Judging my uncomfortable reaction, he gave me a confused look.

"Myyyyy sister's wedding's this weekend," he explained.

"That's right!" I sighed. "Katelyn, your older sister. I think she sent us a wedding invitation a few months ago."

I was so grateful his question had nothing to do with me. If being cursed to control nature's consequences wasn't enough to scare Merritt away, surely the idea of me shopping for wedding dresses would have been something worthy of freaking him out.

"She's gone absolutely insane," he vented as he poked the food on his plate. "My sister has somehow transformed into an evil, angry creature destroying everything that comes in her path. It's hilarious to watch. I have never seen anything like it."

He went on to tell the story about how the family bridezilla had managed to yell, cry, and apologize four separate times in one afternoon.

"You are coming, right?" he asked as we finished our food and headed back to the school.

"I'll go if you want me there."

"Great. Then it's a date."

I smiled. *The* Merritt Emerson asked if I would be his official wedding date. The stars were aligning.

The afternoon sun gleamed through my bedroom window as I stood in front of the mirror getting ready. The room was filled with the soothing fragrance of freshly blow-dried hair and perfume. My long curls hung over my shoulder as I tilted my head to slip in my dangling earrings.

"Five minutes!" I heard my mom yell from downstairs.

I thought that this still counted as a wedding date with Merritt, even though my entire family was attending. And I guessed I would be sitting by myself through the ceremony since he would be one of the groomsmen. But I figured it still counted for something.

I stood up tall and examined my appearance one last time. My hands tugged at my dress to straighten out the creases and I wiped a small smudge of mascara from the corner of my eye.

A text waited unopened on my phone from Merritt. I grinned and picked it up. "The bride has had two meltdowns since we've arrived at the hall. Save me."

Snatching my heels and handbag off the edge of my bed, I started downstairs.

Flutes and stringed instruments filled the air with music as we took our seats in the ribbon-covered rows of white chairs by the vineyard. The seats slowly filled as the guests made their way toward the ceremony location. Towers of wedding gifts filled the back tables as people continued to file in.

Beside me, little Harrison bounced his too short legs that failed to reach the ground. He tugged at his collar and squirmed in his chair, searching for anything to keep him entertained. I was able to grab the wedding program fan out of his hands just before he used it as a weapon to slam over my head.

The music changed, and conversations cut off in unison. Behind us, bridesmaids and groomsmen coupled together made their way down the aisle. The ladies shined in their unique styles of cream-colored, lace dresses with matching brown boots. The groomsmen complemented their outfits with vests and ties of brown and cream.

The groom centered himself in front of the congregation and stared at his shoes. He lightly bounced from side to side, anxious to start the service. His uneasiness wasn't from being nervous. He seemed full of excitement.

The crowd stood up like a subtle ocean wave as I caught a glimpse of a wedding gown in the distance.

I had never really had the chance to get to know Merritt's older sister while growing up. Katelyn was very social and usually running to a friend's house or party whenever I visited. From what I did know of her, she had an extremely likeable personality.

I'm sure Merritt would have loved to have more memories of the two of them, but their relationship seemed to be a little distant. I wondered if she avoided being home to escape the memories of her deceased father.

She looked remarkable as she made her way down the aisle. Her structure was flawless like a perfectly sculpted work of art. She shared her mother's beautiful, green eyes that seemed magnified by the surrounding scenery of rolling green hills and vineyards. As she moved closer, I couldn't help but draw my attention to the handsome man escorting her.

I stood puzzled. With her father out of the picture, I wondered who was filling in for her escort on her wedding day. After a moment, I recognized that this stunning man was my wedding date. Merritt walked, arm and arm with his big sister, as she made her way toward her fiancé at the front of the aisle.

Merritt caught my eye and winked as he walked by. The sight of him so finely dressed melted my heart. I grabbed the back of my chair to steady my dizziness. He looked absolutely breathtaking.

After the ceremony, the crowd shuffled their way indoors to the banquet hall. Merritt came up behind me and grabbed my hand, introducing me to family and acquaintances as we made our way inside. He smiled confidently and smoothly socialized with everyone he saw, pleasing all he came in contact with.

I gazed up at the hanging lanterns and twinkling lights. The tables were adorned with candles and glass vases complementing the background walls frosted with flowers.

Once the two of us found a seat at my family's table, Harrison clung to Merritt like a little puppy. They ended up folding an old candy wrapper and flicking it back and forth across the tablecloth like a paper football.

The night shifted into magical memories as glasses chimed and loved ones enjoyed each other's company. I sat and soaked in the happiness filling the entire room.

There was something extra special about weddings. It was a chance to overlook all of the weaknesses of a flawed couple and celebrate the fact that, no matter the circumstances, two human beings cared for each other greatly and shared a love that they refused to break.

Song after song played on the dance floor. Merritt loosened his tie while we twirled and laughed, surrounded by crowds of people bouncing to the music. We remained on the dance floor as the melody transitioned from fast to a slow, steady tempo.

Merritt pulled me in and rested my hand on his chest. I looked closely into his eyes as our faces lightly touched while we swayed back and forth.

A line of flower girls sat on the floor, resting their elbows on their knees, adoring the paired off couples and the radiant bride and groom. The older folks watched and smiled from their seats, reflecting on how quickly the years had flashed by.

I looked over at Katelyn and her new husband dancing as she gently rested her head on his shoulder. Her wedding ring sparkled in the dim lighting as she held to the back of his neck.

"They look so happy," I said under my breath and turned back to Merritt. He gave me that same look as he did the day behind the waterfall, like he wanted me to know something. He tightened his bottom lip, almost as if he was biting it from the inside, squeezed my hand, and smiled.

As the song ended, the voice of the nearby DJ spoke deeply through the speakers. "Can I get all the married couples to please step onto the dance floor?"

The crowd lightly laughed, and partners of all ages began to stand up. Even the people who had sat in the back through the entire night came forward to participate.

We left the dance floor and took our seats back at the family table. I grabbed a cool glass of ice water and felt refreshed as the condensation on the glass wet my fingers.

Couples danced as the lyrics to the music flowed through the large room.

Afraid and alone, from the dark sleep you saved me.
The dust-lit stars in your eyes had enslaved me.
From that moment on was when I knew
To the deepest of oceans I'd follow you

We walked barefoot on the untouched earth
Like our untouched souls as this new love birthed.
Our dreams became one, one flesh, one bone.
I'd follow you through the fog of unknown.

I looked over and saw Harrison lying fast asleep across two chairs next to my handbag. Looking through the crowd of married couples, I spotted my mom and dad dancing in the background. I watched as my father held my mother's hand to his lips and kissed it. My eyes watered as Mom leaned in and pressed her lips against my dad's temple.

I remember when you cried,
Afraid that I would say goodbye.
Empty paradise,
Cold and blue.
Into the darkness I'll follow you.

Over the music the DJ announced "Any couples who have been married for less than two hours please leave the dance floor." Everyone chuckled as the bride and groom dropped their heads and made their way toward the tables to take a seat.

The DJ continued excusing couples from the dance floor as the song carried on.

"All couples married less than five years, please take your seats."

People gradually trickled back to their tables scattered throughout the room.

"Less than ten years."

"Thirty years."

My parents sat and joined us, and my mother took my hand in hers. By the time the DJ reached fifty years, only one elderly couple was left standing. The old man's frail hands held his wife's tightly as they slowly rocked back and forth in the middle of the room. Her eyes sparkled as she looked back at him proudly. I could tell as I watched them that at that moment, no one else in the room existed.

I'll hold you close inside my arms
And fall into the icy storms.
With you with me will be enough.
We'll find the light beneath the rough.

In the corner of my eye, I saw tears glisten on my mother's cheeks. She studied the dancing couple and longed to know every microscopic detail flowing through the hourglass of their lives. They were a symbol of perseverance. Together they had pushed through all of their challenges and held on through the good and the bad, constantly moving forward.

I reflected on how precious life was and felt guilty for everything I had ever taken for granted. Especially time. I thought of Mom and her cancer, how it was sucking her hours and minutes away. No matter how many countless times I endeavored to use my gift, the powers inside me would retreat and refuse to push in her direction to save her. I didn't know how long she had left and thought of the moments I had with her that I would never get back.

Then I looked over at Merritt. My heart warmed, and I suddenly recognized the emotions I was feeling as he looked back at me. It was the same sensation I felt toward everything in my life that was precious to me but to a much stronger degree. It was the feeling I related to the woods, to music, to my family, to Shyler, to Beck, to this wedding, to laughter, to happiness. It was love.

The music echoed in my ears, and the candlelight reflected in the corners of Merritt's eyes. He pulled me away from the ticking rush of time, and we froze in the moment while everything else around us stood still.

I grabbed his hand and led him out of the banquet room. The music continued to muffle through the insulated walls as I led him into the emergency staircase down the hallway.

I leaned against the large, glass window and pulled him in closer. He slowly stepped toward me and dropped his hands to my sides.

I closed my eyes and let my mind go as he leaned in and kissed me. My hands grabbed his loose tie and gently pulled his face in closer. The mouthwatering taste of his lips gently fluttered at the tip of my tongue. His warm hand reached up and slid against the side of my neck as his thumb lightly caressed the corner of my mouth.

The dizziness of life faded away around me. My thoughts were simple. I loved Merritt. I couldn't remember another moment like this when I could translate my emotions so clearly. I was a young schoolgirl watching my heart stand at the front of the classroom and write the answers on the chalkboard in plain sight. He had become my everything.

In the background, we heard the music end as the DJ announced that it was time to cut the cake. Merritt pulled back his head and smiled. He kissed me once more and led me back inside.

I paused for a brief second and turned to glance out the staircase window. The lighted hallway made it impossible to see anything in the darkness outside, but I felt a sudden strange sensation. Someone was out there, looking in. I brushed it off and turned back to Merritt.

By the time we made it back to the reception hall, the air had filled with giddiness and excitement. We hurried and made our way back to our table.

"All right, ladies. Put your game faces on. It's time for the bouquet toss," the DJ laughed.

I slumped down in my seat, hoping that no one noticed my choice not to participate. All the small flower girls went skipping up to the front, joined by a trail of young, single women. As they huddled together, Merritt and my mother pushed me out of my seat, urging me to take part in the fun.

Unenthusiastically, I hurried to the middle and waited as the girls around me giggled and stretched out their arms to gain the flower catching advantage.

At the front of the room, Katelyn motioned for everyone to spread out, then spun around with the back of her dress facing the group of girls.

As she gripped the bouquet, ready to let it fly, I scanned the room and spotted the shadowed face of a wedding guest walking through the doorway. This stranger was casually dressed with his tie loosened and rolled up sleeves under a faded gray vest. Then I froze when I recognized those bright blue eyes and shaved head. He nodded toward me as he slowly strutted along the back wall.

Hot sweat pasted to my neck as the room began spinning around me. I had never seen his face in real life, but I knew in that instant, he had finally found me.

He slowly walked between the tables of laughing guests without breaking eye contact with me and made his way toward the table with Merritt and my family.

The flowers flew through the air.

My eyes were glued to the man as he came up and hovered behind my mother. Discreetly, his hand slipped down and clung to her shoulder. I saw my mom suddenly turn white and grab the back of the chair to her side. Her glass slipped out of her hand and shattered on the floor at the exact same moment the wedding bouquet fell to the ground and landed at my feet.

My dad bolted up and ran around the table to my mother as she dropped to the floor, too distracted to notice the strange man beside her. Everyone nearby quickly stood up and gathered around her in a tight crowd. I heard Merritt yell for someone to call an ambulance.

"Mom!" My eyes began to swell up with tears. As I looked back to the doorway the man from the mirror had slipped away.

Chapter 17

H ow is she?"

"They have her at the medical center in Portland," I explained to Shyler. "It's pretty bad. I'll go see her again on Wednesday." She rested her hand on my shoulder, rubbing it lightly.

Mom had insisted on us leaving her there by herself for a few days so we didn't trouble ourselves with the tiring commute over and over again. As hard as Dad had tried to stay, she had strongly insisted so he could get some real sleep in a comfortable bed at home.

"I'm sure everything will be fine," Shyler said.

Mr. Craven stood at the front of the classroom reviewing assignments and answering questions for tomorrow's exam. The light of the overhead projector reflected against his tiny glasses as he scribbled notes in his impossible-to-read penmanship.

"Mr. Craven, can we review the Zumba chapter again?" Addison interrupted from the back row.

"You mean Karma?"

"Whatever," she replied and rolled her eyes.

Lane's hand shot up from the back of the classroom.

"I can explain, Craves." He shifted back and slouched

in his chair, giving off the look of confidence and complete relaxation. Just the sound of his slimy voice made my throat tighten to avoid revisiting my lunch.

Mr. Craven nodded his head. "Go ahead, Lane. And . . . stop calling me Craves."

Lane's eyes shifted in my direction. I watched him trace the dark scar now surrounding his stubby index finger from the night I had bitten him.

"Bad karma could be like when a guy approaches a chick. He's actually doing her more of a favor than anything, since he's way out of her league in the first place, and she somehow refuses him. Then bad things start to happen to her. It's probably karma telling her she messed up rejecting him, right?"

The whole class began to snicker.

"Yeah, Mr. Craven, like really bad things end up happening to her," Addison added. "I'm serious. Her mom will probably die like any day. It doesn't get much unluckier than that."

Their words directed at me felt like a punch to the face. Something reached inside of me and pulled down on my heart, sinking it deeper and deeper into a black hole.

I quickly stood up.

"Be right back," I whispered to Shy as I pulled my seat back.

"Are you all right?"

"I'll be fine. Just need some air."

"Is there a problem, Miss Perry?" Mr. Craven asked, clearly upset by the distraction.

"I'm sorry. I'll just be a minute." I slipped out of the classroom without giving him a chance to respond.

As I entered the bathroom, I encountered the shy girl I had sat by in the lunchroom. I hadn't seen her since the day the bully had kicked my soda bottle. As she washed her hands by the sink, I tried to flash a half smile to hide my emotions. I walked into the closest stall and sank behind the door.

Almost immediately, tears began streaming down my face. I covered my mouth with both hands to silence my crying. I waited until it was quiet, knowing the girl had left the restroom. Then I gasped for air between my breathy cries to make up for the earlier lack of oxygen.

Ever since I had learned about my mother's brain tumor, I continuously tried to push it away. There was no preparation for what might happen, and I felt the weight of everything engulf me, burying me alive. I wasn't ready to lose her.

I blinked to squeeze out the salty tears blurring my vision. Across from me, on the opposite wall, I saw etched in letters:

Annie loves David.

Even though it was surrounded by countless, similar markings, that particular spot intrigued me. The delicate care exercised in the carving defended its treasured space on the wall. I felt like the message of that single relationship was completely and genuinely true. Whoever this Annie was, I believed she did love a boy named David with all her heart.

My mind retraced the memory from Katelyn's wedding, and I pictured the elderly couple alone on the dance floor. I remembered my mother enraptured by their affection. In all those wonderful years of marriage they had shared together, perhaps there were times that weren't so wonderful. After that amount of time, they had to have experienced horrible trials and losses of their own.

Maybe the sadness I was feeling was common and eventually happened to everyone. Perhaps it was the hard times that made them look so beautiful and unified as they danced in each other's arms. Their life was a mysterious recipe of ingredients, good and bad, that painted an excellent existence.

Five minutes must have passed as I concentrated on the simple words scraped on the wall in front of me before I realized I had stopped crying.

Chapter 18

A mist of fog came seeping through the hillside, covering the lower part of town. The glow from the clouded sun lit up the gorge in a pale shade of glacier blue. Although the fog wasn't thick enough to affect my driving, I turned on the headlights as extra caution for oncoming traffic.

On the sides of the road, naked trees from fallen leaves reached out toward me with an eerie vibe. Through the tree lining, I could see a dead, yellow valley of dry grass clumped with wet mud and mossy weeds. The fog stretched across the field like an ocean of rippling white foam and crept over the roots of the tangled tree trunks as it smeared out across the road.

My eyes caught a glimpse of a dark, still figure as I sped by. I looked over, startled to recognize the withered, old, hermit woman standing in the middle of the lifeless meadow.

Fear struck inside me, and I gasped as I saw her haunting eyes staring straight back.

My sight pulled away a little too late as the road began to curve. The car continued straight, skidding over the shoulder, then rumbled through the side gravel.

I screamed as I slammed on the brakes and stopped the car inches before hitting a fence-post off the highway. My heart pounded in my chest, and my lungs choked for tiny breaths of air as I attempted to calm my frantic nerves.

I looked out the back window. Behind me she stood watching. Even though I feared her, I knew I had to approach her. She held answers to my unsettled questions, and they stirred inside me as if trapped in an uncomfortable wool sweater in the dripping heat of summer.

My hands shook while I scrambled to unbuckle my seatbelt. I stepped out of the car and stomped and slid through the mud toward the woman in the distance.

She stood motionless and waited. Her stillness made me uneasy, like a poisonous spider waiting patiently for its prey to stumble into its inescapable web.

I stopped far enough away to allow a large gap between us, remaining out of danger.

"What happened to my mother?" I asked, trying to control my escaping breath.

There was no need to explain my question in greater detail. I sensed that she was aware of all that had happened to me.

"The man who comes for you can take from others their energy and life, like a wild, blood-sucking bat with no care for anything but its own survival. If one were weak, it wouldn't take much to send them to their grave."

The air trembled in the back of my throat. I was not the only one with gifts and what this man was capable of could be lethal to those I loved.

A twig snapped behind me. I quickly turned to the sound, but saw nothing. When I looked forward again, the witch had vanished.

In a brief moment, I felt her intimate presence as she

leaned in from behind me and whispered in my ear, "You haven't much time. She is slipping. You must go to her now."

A gust of icy air rushed past my face as I searched for the witch in every direction, but I found myself alone in the marshy field.

I sprinted back to the car and made an immediate U-turn, heading toward the highway that led to Portland. I had to get to my mother immediately.

The sound of my shoes echoed against the white walls of the long hallway as I made my way to the farthest hospital room. Each fluorescent light above me buzzed to a different musical pitch as they beamed down on my face.

As I passed by each cracked open door, I captured a glimpse of every patient and their unique atmospheres. I was granted a flicker into each individual's private life. B-22 . . . lonely. B-24 . . . inconsolable. B-26 . . . a glimmer of hope. B-28 . . . defeated.

When I approached the last room, my pace dramatically decelerated. I wished that if I slowed down enough I would never have to face what waited inside. Perhaps not facing it meant it didn't exist. If I turned around now I could run away, and none of this unhappiness had to happen.

I glanced up at the ceiling where a rounded mirror bubbled out of the corner of the wall. My morphed reflection grew wider and sharpened with each bitter step I took.

The doorway welcomed me all too quickly. I rounded up all of the courage inside me to continue moving forward.

As I peeked in I saw my mother sleeping. Her pale skin matched the light tint of the stiff bed sheets. The glow of bright energy that always surrounded her had faded into almost nothing.

In contrast to her lifeless tone, the hospital room was inundated with vases of colorful flowers, finger painted pictures, and heartfelt "Get well" cards from family and loved ones. The gifts and decorations poured out slivers of hope to heal her failing core.

I reached down and held a crayon picture from Harrison of Mom in a smudged superhero cape, flying high over the mountains. The colorful wax displayed a giant, crooked smile across her face.

I focused on the evidence of the lives she had touched and examined each gift, trying to ignore the distracting background of needles, monitors, and medical tubes threatening to unravel my thread of hopefulness.

Although it was painful to watch her lying in the hospital bed, I also noticed a peaceful simplicity that swaddled my thoughts like a crinkled candy wrapper. In front of me was this sweet individual who found goodness in everything she came in contact with. I had watched her my whole life, but I had never *seen* her until this very moment.

She was a pebble dropped in still water. As small as she was, her kindness and love rippled out in every direction until it touched everything. She was so beautiful. The life she lived was beautiful.

My eyes suddenly felt wet. I dried them with the tip of my sleeve and walked over to the sink for a drink of water to clear my empty throat. The stuffy air of the room clogged my nose with the smell of damp walls and humidity.

I made my way back to the bedside and held my mother's hand. The touch of my warm palms woke her from her quiet sleep. She shifted her head in my direction and struggled to open her heavy eyes.

"Hi, baby," she whispered. I forced a smile across my face, silently rubbing her hand. As she tried adjusting the shoulders of her green hospital gown to get comfortable, I could see the pain with every movement she made.

"Is anyone else here?"

"Just me. Everyone else is driving down later this week. I was able to sneak away early."

She closed her tired eyes for a moment. I could sense her slowly pulling away from me, and it broke my heart to watch.

I still wasn't ready to say goodbye to her. There was a selfish fear inside of me. It was as if I were the victim being buried deep in a hole of blackness. I wanted to shout at the top of my lungs for someone to come to the rescue and pull me up and into the light and take away this burden so I would never lose her.

My mom squeezed my hand as tightly as her frail strength would allow her. "Ry, I need you to do something for me."

"Anything, Mom. I promise."

The pen in her hands trembled as she signed the hospital discharge forms.

"Are you sure you want to be released right now, Mrs. Perry? The doctor strongly advises against it," the nurse behind the desk reminded her.

Mom looked straight into her eyes and smiled.

"I understand and I really appreciate your concern, but I need to do this," she replied, and we turned to leave the lobby.

A nurse pushed her wheel chair and rolled her out the double doors to the parking lot, since she had become too weak to stand for long on her own.

An older man approaching the doors in front of us

gracefully hurried to hold it open and waited for us to pass through. He smiled and wished us a good day.

I unlocked my power with ease allowing natural goodness to glide toward the man. With the exception of my mother, it was becoming less and less difficult to unleash the vessel inside me. Karma flowed comfortably through my bones like I was literally holding a doorknob and twisting it open and closed in complete control. As the old man walked away, I felt assured that the loved one he was coming to visit was feeling well and rapidly recovering.

I ran and pulled the car around and parked at the curb. Slowly, Mom and the nurse inched toward the passenger's side and Mom dropped tenderly into the seat. The nurse smiled and helped her buckle her seatbelt then left the two of us alone.

"Are you sure you don't want to go home?" I asked, hoping she would change her mind.

"We only have a little while before the sun sets and I'm running out of time, Rylee. Please, you promised." Her voice sounded so weak as it struggled to break through her vocal chords.

I began driving west. As we left the busy hustling freeways of Portland, the roads became quieter, and we were able to soak in the rolling hills and open fields around us, letting go of our center-staged troubles.

The driving time passed too quickly, and before I knew it, I began spotting road signs that led to the beach. They triggered memories of my childhood trips to the coast that were tucked away in the back closets of my mind. I remembered building sand castles with baby Harrison and boogie boarding the shallow waves with my dad.

The images flickered and jumped back even further, before Harrison was born. I saw my mom, young and beautiful, sunbathing in her red, striped swimsuit with bright, glamorous lipstick. I ran to her crying from the pain of the beach sand in my eyes. She smiled her comforting smile and held me, dabbing away the sand with the corner of her beach towel.

"Right down there's perfect, Rylee." Mom pointed to an abandoned beach nook. I parked the car as close to her desired destination as possible and turned off the engine.

Quickly, I ran around to grab an old, thick wool blanket from the trunk and draped it around mother's shoulders as she struggled to pull herself from the car seat.

She leaned on my shoulder as we stepped together over the large rocks until we reached the sandy shore of the beach. We found a steep sand dune facing the shore where we could sit and watch the water roll in and back out to the ocean.

Mom trembled as I tucked the blanket around us and adjusted our position so she could lie comfortably. Once she was able to relax she took in a deep breath of fresh, salty air and stared out at the water in satisfied silence.

The foamy waves crept over the glittering sand floor and stretched their fingers to touch as much land as they could before being pulled back to their watery arena down below. The soft white noise of the crashing waves surrounded us in peace as tightly as the blue blanket wrapped around our bodies.

Tears filled her eyes as she watched the neon orange sun fade beneath the distant waves. A small flock of seagulls skipped across the wet sand, following the shallow water out to sea.

"I'm gonna miss this," she whispered. "There is so much beauty in everything."

Pressing her lips together, I could see them tremble as she fought back the urge to sob.

I sat beside her without saying a word. It wasn't fair that she was sick. *Why can't I protect her? I am a balancer. This is what I am meant for!*

I shut my eyelids tightly and focused intently on the storm inside me. The powers bounced against my inner walls, fighting to be let out, but they seemed blocked by an unseen shield surrounding me. Not me, surrounding Mom. The harder I fought, the more the energy magnetized back against me and drained my inner strength.

Why isn't it working? My mom's entire life she had submerged others with kindness. Every second she breathed she was focused on helping anyone but herself. And now, when she needed a miracle the most, my gift was unable to save her.

It didn't make sense that so much good could be allowed to vanish from this world when so much unhappiness was happening all around us.

"Why do bad things have to happen to good people?" I finally asked.

Mom's eyes lit up as she immediately answered, "Because if there was no bad, you wouldn't recognize that the good is good. Without horrible, you would have no fantastic. YOU have always been my fantastic, Rylee."

She reached up a gentle hand and brushed back the hair that slid into my face.

"My life has been perfect in every way," she continued, "I have received so much more than my fair share of goodness. I wouldn't ask for anything more or change a single thing."

Maybe this was the hidden shield that blocked my power. I realized that Mom's life was already balanced. She had appreciated every shred of goodness that she was granted, and the justifying energy was unable to pour more over a soul satisfied with its good fortune and happiness.

But I couldn't think about the good. All I could think about was how horrible it was that all of this was happening.

I thought of the villainous man in the mirror. A lump formed in my throat as I thought of his offer and his threat, telling me others around me would get hurt. He had warned me. It was him who had made her weak, pulling out the last of her living energy with his power, but I felt responsible.

"I'm sorry for my mistakes, Mom," I said softly.

She put an arm around me and squeezed as tightly as her strength would allow.

"I am so proud of the woman you have become, Rylee. And I love you more than anything." She brought her hand up and touched the side of my chin, examining my face.

"You are a special person. There is something magnificent you were meant to do in this world. I can feel it," she said.

Up close, she looked so fragile. Her white, chapped lips wrinkled when she spoke and thick, dark circles puffed out underneath her eyes.

"Search out the sunlight in everything, Rylee. There will always be moments of greatness in life that make all the bad worth it."

I held her closer and forced my eyes shut to fight back the unstoppable tears. "I'm not ready to say goodbye."

I began to sob. We both wept in each other's arms and the tears that fell from our faces soaked into the brightly patterned wool blanket.

Mother wiped the wetness from under her eyes. "I will always be right there. You know I will never leave you."

I was soothed by her words. A warm tingling inside reassured me that the things she spoke were true.

"I love you, Mom. So much. Thank you for everything."

I held her close and watched as her chest moved up and down, each time becoming slower and slower. My eyes never looked away as we sat in silence for what must have been hours. Her grip on my hand softly loosened, and I watched her breathe in and out for the very last time.

My heart recognized that she was gone, but my head refused to believe it.

"Mom?"

There was no answer, and a moment passed by.

"Mom?" I repeated. Not a sound.

I refused. I waited. Water began to fill the lining of my eyelids again.

I whispered to her, begging, "Mom, please don't go." But she had already left.

My heart went ice cold. The tears in my eyes were now endlessly streaming. My lungs wanted to climb out of my chest, desperate for air.

I felt my entire world collapse inside of my mind. All around me the thick stone walls of security I had spent my entire existence relying upon crumbled into dust. Never had I felt more lost. I was a speck, dropped into the darkness of an entirely new universe, and the idea of making it back to the home I knew was impossible.

Not knowing what else to do and with no ability to think, I held my mom tighter. Her hand was still clutched firmly in mine. I searched all around me, panicking to find someone nearby to help, and suddenly found myself looking up.

I stared at the stars, and they burned brighter and brighter as my watery eyes began to clear up and focus. With everything that was churning rapidly through my head, I was able to stop and complete one single thought for a moment.

The stars are beautiful.

A veil was uncovered from my eyes and while I was unable to grasp understanding, I felt full and overtaken with the beauty. Although my mom had taken her journey elsewhere and departed from my life, she had left me with a fragile impression of comprehension.

I realized my mother had a gift too. She could see. She could find the beauty in absolutely everything.

Chapter 19

I drifted, lost, herded through a pack of solemn, teary faces. Black dresses and button-up shirts encircled mother's casket. I read and reread the words written across her tombstone.

IN MEMORY OF EVELYN PERRY
WHO SAW THE SUNLIGHT IN EVERYTHING

A gentleman in a clean cut suit stood up in front of the multitude and spoke words of comfort to anyone willing to listen. Although his desire to console was sincere, my heart became numb to his words. They bounced off my chest without breaking through to my emotions.

I muted everything out and stared with tunnel vision as they lowered her into the ground. The anxiety began creeping deep inside of me, and I felt trapped in an invisible globe with the glass walls quickly shrinking smaller and smaller.

I turned my back to the coffin and began walking, leaving it far behind me. I caught a glimpse of Merritt's concerned face in the crowd as I left, but he stood still, allowing me this moment to sort things out alone.

I paced through the rows of mysterious tombstones

and began counting them. How many people lay here in eternal sleep forgotten? These names meant nothing to me, and I shivered thinking of others in years to come who would walk past my mother's grave and think of her as only a meaningless number, never knowing the angelic person she had been when she was alive.

That brief interaction and gentle touch of their encountering fingerprints would fade into nothing. They would never learn of her journey and gleaming personality. After glancing at her name they would continue walking by and she would casually dissolve from their world like strangers bumping shoulders in a crowded subway.

The headstones overlooked the river from the grassy hillside. I watched Harrison from a distance skipping rocks across the water then gazed out at the drifting clouds floating by at a leisurely pace; their reflection sliding across the wet surface without friction to disturb the gentle waves.

We drove home after the ceremony without a single word exchanged in the car. I leaned my head against the backrest and listened for Mom's sweet voice to start up a conversation to end the long silence, but her words never came. I got out of the car, but instead of following Harrison and Dad inside, I took off into the woods.

I followed the familiar path up the hillside without stopping until I reached the old, run-down hut. Tears streamed down my face as I stood and stared blankly at the place where it had all begun.

I wanted to destroy it and all the events that had followed since that day I had stumbled upon the hermit. Rage flowed from the top of my head all the way down to my toes. My mind shook inside my skull ready to burst. I fell to my knees and covered my ears, screaming and wailing. I wanted to explode into a thousand pieces.

Looking down by my shoes, I found a big, jagged stone. I quickly scrambled back up to my feet and chucked it as hard as I could at the shack and screamed out in anger.

Scanning the ground, I proceeded to throw more rocks. I was convinced if I continued long enough I could use up every ounce of my strength and escape the torment. Perhaps then the pain inside would shrivel up into silent echoed memories.

Running out of energy, I finally collapsed to the ground trying to catch my breath and control my crying. My arms cupped my gut, attempting to clutch the inconsolable feelings spilling out of my core. They poured out of me until there was nothing left and then some, as if my emotions were dry heaving out of my heart.

A sudden burning in the back of my skull tingled and warned me that I was no longer alone. I turned back to see a lingering figure hiding in the trees. The witch was watching from the shadows of the thick forest.

Her haunting face would normally cause my stomach to tighten and my hands to tremble, but I was emotionally drained. There was no room for fear in my heart. It had withered and dried into a dying autumn leaf.

"What do you want from me?" I mumbled under my breath. Only a moment flashed before I could feel her presence close, hovering right behind me.

"It is not I, but he who desires something of yours." She spoke of the man in the mirror.

"Who is he?" I asked, too weak and numb to do anything but stare forward.

"He is my brother."

My eyes narrowed, and I turned to face her. How was that even possible? She seemed old enough to be his grandmother.

She answered my question before giving me the chance to ask, "He regains his youth through the energy in the lives he soaks up around him. We can choose to give or take life from others."

"We?" I asked, perplexed.

She slowly squatted down beside me and plucked a bright red poppy hiding under a small pile of rocky dirt. I watched as she delicately cupped it in her weathered hand. She focused on its detail and handled it with deep appreciation.

As she deeply inhaled, the soft petals slowly began to crumble before my eyes. It shriveled into nothing until all that was left were pieces of a dried stem. She stretched out her fingers and the dust was swept away in the soft breeze.

"For years we searched for it together until it became an incurable obsession. We were explorers journeying across the world starving for answers, like a treasure map of immeasurable value. After all our research, we were sure we'd be the first to find it. It consumed my brother and changed him into something dark."

"It took you years to find what?" I had so many questions stirring in my mind.

"The tree of life," she smiled. It was the first time I had ever seen her rotting, crooked teeth. And for a moment, I caught a glimpse of cheerfulness in her mysterious disposition.

"Wait," I questioned her in disbelief. "The Tree of Life? Like from the Garden of Eden?"

She nodded.

I thought back to my religions class and our unit on the book of Genesis. Sitting next to Shyler, I was burdened with meaningless facts constantly babbling from her lips. She was fascinated with the Old Testament and had plenty of input to share from her early morning seminary classes before school.

"There is no way," I told the old woman. "That's just . . . how is that possible?"

"We never reached the tree or ate of the actual fruit. But what we discovered instead was equally as satisfying"

She reached down to the same area where she had grabbed the hidden flower and touched the spot where it was earlier planted.

"The life of the tree flowed through its roots. Those roots dug deep into a stream under the Earth that came out at a hidden fountain."

Before I had a chance to react, she reached up her hands and covered my eyes.

I was taken by vision deep into a thick jungle. It was hot and sticky. The humidity felt almost unbearable. The setting screeched with the buzzing and howling of countless varieties of nearby wildlife.

I watched a man and a woman trekking through the trees, weighed down with hiking gear. By the looks of their canvas pouched backpacks and old leather boots, I must have been taken almost a century back in time.

I recognized the tall man. How could I forget the person who had come for my mother? He wore a sweaty bandana covering his smooth, hairless scalp.

He walked beside a stunningly beautiful woman. Her long, yellow braids swayed from side to side with each step she took along the jungle trail. She slapped a giant bug that landed on her bare shoulder and wiped her sticky hand at her side.

"Remind me again, Nathaniel, why we left our comfortable life back in New York to find this tree without hiring a team of experienced guides? It would have made this trip much more efficient," she said as she stopped to catch her breath.

"No one else is to know the location when we find it," the man snapped back. "Once we learn if the legends are true, if the fruit can make a human forever immortal, then we can decide what to do with that information."

The woman eyed him with a hint of distrust. "I don't see a point in being the first to discover something if it's kept a secret." The man paced forward, ignoring her arguing comment.

They soon came across a crystal clear stream flowing into a deep pool of water. The woman cupped both hands into the pool and began to wash her face in the refreshing, cool stream. She leaned back on her hands and stared straight up into the sky. Drops of water fell from her face and her eyes.

The man studied a map, muttering under his breath and cursing in frustration. "We've been searching for days, going in circles! It should be right here!" I could see the greed in his eyes and the longing for their long awaited treasure.

Nearby, a tall wall of leeching brush and stone towered above them. The natural fence stretched out along the side of the stream endlessly in each direction. The man started exploring their roadblock, looking for a vulnerable section to climb and get a better view of their unfamiliar surroundings.

Suddenly, the woman began screaming in terror, scratching at her eyes. She fell backwards and thrashed against the hard ground.

"I can't see, Nathaniel! I'm blind! I'M BLIND!" There must have been something toxic in the water she had just washed her face in.

The man ran over to her and pulled her away from the

pool. He held her in his arms and looked into her eyes.

"Sister, don't panic," he tried to calm her.

"Nathaniel," she cried. "I can't see you. I can't see!"

As she struggled to open her eyes, I began to recognize her face. Underneath her young beauty, I identified the eyes of the hermit woman. This was the moment she had lost her sight.

Time escaped me again, and I experienced another quick flash forward into the vision. In the same location the brother, Nathaniel, I suppose this was his name, and his sister slept by their knapsacks in the darkness of the jungle.

The woman's eyes were covered in white bandages. She suddenly sat up and lifted the cloth covering her face. Her eyes were glowing that smoky familiar shade of white I had always known.

She rose from her bed and began walking toward the water. Her face looked as though it was gazing up the hill in the far distance.

"Nathaniel, wake up," she whispered.

Nathaniel immediately became alert and quickly came to her side. She pointed far in the distance.

"There it is!" she exclaimed. "I see the tree."

His eyes squinted as he tried to adjust to the darkness. "I see nothing."

"What do you mean? It's right there, bright and glowing. It is the Tree of Life. Exactly the same as our research! It's so beautiful."

She dropped down to her knees, overwhelmed.

"There's nothing there! It's just a stretch of stone and jungle vines!" Nathaniel looked over at his sister and saw her glossy eyes focusing intently on what she believed lay in the distance.

"It's there, Nathaniel. I see . . . I see . . ." A single tear streamed down her cheek. "I see the water."

He watched as his blind sister stumbled in the darkness and came again to the pool of water that had taken away her sight.

"It glows white and pure just like the tree," she whispered.

Frustrated that he wasn't able to see what she saw, she began to weep. Nathaniel knelt beside her and held her shoulders. He was calmer now, more gentle than before.

She reached up her hands and felt the skin on his face, trying to recognize the shapes of his features. Her fingers glided from his lips to his cheekbones and slowly up to his eyes. Just as her skin touched the lids of his eyes, he recoiled back and shrieked.

"What was that?" he yelled. His face iced over in disbelief. "Do it again, cover my eyes!"

She pressed her hands against his eyes, and he saw a bright tree glowing in the distance behind the stonewall. Its brightness sparkled like a clustered galaxy of shooting stars. Below the roots, glimmering water trickled down through the towering wall and streamed out to the pool beside them.

Nathaniel broke away from his sister's fingers and raced into the darkness to the blockade. He began tearing branches and bushes violently; searching for a way in and halted when he reached a hidden doorway. The entrance was sealed, impossible to break open, even with the finest of tools.

He began pounding against the rock door frantically and cursing. Blood from his damaged hands stained the door and he stopped when he noticed a faded symbol burnt into the rock. It was an ancient pictograph of a body holding two circles. One balanced in each hand perfectly. Nathaniel calmed himself and caressed the symbol with his bloody finger. Backing away from the wall in defeat, he knelt back down beside his sister.

He cupped his hand in the fountain, examining where the light once radiated from the clear ripples. The scratches from beating against the stone began to rapidly heal in front of his eyes like magic.

"What is this water?" he whispered.

As he reached in again, the woman still gazed into nothingness, examining the breathtaking tree. She had stumbled upon her new gift by accident from the stream, now able to see past the veil of mortality into parallel worlds.

Her eyes traced the sparkling water again. Deep under the pool a dark figure clouded the waves of light. She reached her hand down to the pebbled bottom and pulled out a dark, onyx mirror. Its wet surface reflected the concealed world around her, and she could see the surroundings that were limited to her before.

Through the mirror she gazed at Nathaniel's face and was startled by his heartless expression. As his mind churned with his thoughts, she was terrified by the dark energy she saw glowing inside of him.

He suddenly wiped the wetness from the clear water that dripped down his narrow lips.

The scene flashed out of sight, and the witch removed her hands from my eyes. I looked around the familiar scenery of the old, broken shack and looked back down at my black funeral dress.

"You drank from the fountain," I said. "You and your brother received immortality."

She nodded.

"The water could only help us if we stayed there permanently and continuously drank from it. It was our first glances in the mirror that unleashed our ability to soak up living energy in everything around us. After that, my brother hungered for life, feasting on any soul he wanted.

I ran away and left, surviving only on trees and plant life. It leaves me weak and hollow, but I made the choice never to take the life of a human to survive."

The thought of stealing life from others made me shiver. I thought of the moments stolen from my mother and how Nathaniel was using his freshly collected time. My jaw tightened in anger.

"So, if you possess the same power, can't you stop him and somehow take life from him the way he takes from others?" I asked, determined to find a way to eliminate him from existence.

"His strength is much greater. He would kill me before I had the chance to stop him."

I turned away. There had to be a way he could be stopped. I wanted to punish him for what he had done to my mother. If only he had directly hurt me, I could have unleashed all of the power stored inside of me to watch him pay.

The hermit raised her head and closed her eyes, feeling the soft breeze slide past her face.

"I'm sorry about your mother," she whispered.

For some reason, her condolences upset me. I felt like she had no right to apologize for what had happened. Her blood had murdered my blood. I looked down on her, and my heart instinctively began to blame *her* for what had happened.

"If I had never met you, she would still be here," I spoke sharply.

I stood up and stormed away without looking back. Racing through the woods, I tried running from the pain, but the faster I ran, the more tangled in sorrow I felt. Tears began to sting my eyes again.

Chapter 20

As days passed, I felt disconnected from the life I was living. My body became robotic. All the wires and screws moved and functioned correctly, but there was nothing else inside.

My mind had melted like a cube of butter, losing its shape and texture, and dried into a flattened pile of mush. My thoughts had degraded to nothing more than animal instincts. *It's hungry. It's thirsty. It's tired.* My days consisted of wandering from couch to kitchen to bed.

Dad wasn't any different. If I could have remembered how it felt to be conscious of concern for others, I probably would have felt sorry for him. He spent hours gazing out the window without moving.

We exchanged glances like zombies, unaware if the other person staring back indeed existed or not, then looked away, continuing in our individual lives of numbness.

Even Beck had lost all her energy. She would find the darkest corners of the house to hide away in and had no motivation to do anything but sleep.

Harrison had more energy than the rest of us. He still rarely spoke but found ways to keep himself occupied. He would sit on the steps crashing his toy cars silently, and he found places outside to explore on his own.

My back ached from the hours spent curled up on the couch flipping through mind-numbing TV channels. I stretched for the remote and shut off the television.

Reaching for my slippers, I shifted my weight so my feet could fall to the floor in front of me. After sliding them into the woolly soles, I leaned forward resting my elbows on the tops of my knees and cupped my nose and mouth into the palm of my hands.

I felt the warm breath heat up my face and the soothing sensation sparked my slow-moving thoughts. *It's warm like a blanket. Warm blanket. Warm bed. Go up to bed now.*

My legs ached with each step up the creaking stairs. When I reached the top I was stopped at the sight of the closed door to Mom's office workspace. Every day since the funeral I had looked away to avoid the pain, but today my eyes accidentally began to trace its familiar outline out of habit as I stood facing the haunting door.

I took a deep breath and began stepping away, as far against the opposite wall as I could, as if even the risk of touching it would damage me. But with every step I took, my eyes remained glued to her door. When I reached the end of the hall, I gripped the handle to my bedroom door tightly. I was ready to walk away, but my eyes stood prisoner to mother's painting room.

A moment passed, and I couldn't break loose of its clutching spell. I spun around, marched back down the hallway, and shoved open her door.

I'm not sure what I had thought I would find inside, perhaps a dark hole of loneliness or a monstrous creature of gloom lurking in the shadows. But I was surprised to find myself wrapped in no negative emotion.

My eyes circled the studio and studied the details of

Mom's unfinished work. Her piles of scattered paint jars left a lingering feeling of hope and creation. I was overcome with the peace that still simmered and soaked in the walls of the room.

I stepped in and examined everything with fascination. My thumb lightly stroked her glasses tipping sideways on the corner of her desk. I read through her last scribbles and notes on papers and studied stacks of colorful photographs scattered over the shelves.

As I rummaged through her filing cabinet, my fingers marinated in the life that trickled out of the pages of letters and hand sketches buried deep inside. I tried drinking everything in and submerged myself in the evidence of her memories and existence.

As this addiction grew, I felt myself coming alive again. Like a body limb reviving from falling asleep, the tingling sensation dissolved the numbness that days before completely clouded over me.

I traced my fingertips along the border of an old photograph of the family at the beach. Then I pulled out a recent pencil sketch Mom had started of me in the wedding gown we had stumbled upon at the bridal shop.

In the corner of the room, I came across a covered pile of Mom's paintings leaning against the wall. I sat on the floor beside them and began pulling pictures out one by one. There was a beautiful black and white portrait of Harrison as a newborn baby wrapped in one of Dad's old baseball jerseys. I tilted my head to the side to better examine the painting texture, and hidden behind it another picture slipped out through my fingers.

Resting on the floor beside my foot I looked at the dark painting and recognized the face of the witch from the woods. Terror crept inside me as her smoky eyes burned me from the inside out, like they always had.

She was painted sitting on a street corner with a little covered basket clutched tightly in her hands. I recognized the basket from the first day I had met her out in the woods. It had been full of lava rocks she had fumbled through to spark up her stones.

The terrifying painting was smeared in hard, downward strokes. I could picture the surface of the image being violently attacked with a stiff, bristled paintbrush. Although the background was shaded in shadows, her penetrating gaze was crisp and clear.

But this is one of my mom's art pieces. How is that possible? Why does she have a painting of the blind woman who haunted me?

My hands trembled as I reached to the ground and touched the picture. I flipped it over and read my mother's handwriting.

"Esther"

She had dated it the year before I was born. My mind flooded with panic and confusion. Holding the painted picture I sprinted out of the room and ran downstairs into the kitchen.

Dad sat slouched at the table, watching the golden honey on his butter knife puddle onto his cold plate of stale bread rolls.

I slammed down the painting in front of him.

"Why does Mom have this picture?" I yelled.

His miserable expression didn't change as he studied the face in the painting. His hand pressed on the corner of the canvas as he slid it toward him to see it at a better angle.

"Her name was Esther. She was a homeless woman who stumbled into our town before you were born. She probably died a long time ago."

Yeah, probably, unless she happens to be able to suck the

life out of everything around her, giving her the power of immortality, I thought to myself sarcastically.

"How did she know her?" I interrogated.

"It must have been around the holidays. We were out shopping and saw her, such a sad soul, begging on the streets." Dad began to lightly laugh, "You know your mother, always being thoughtful. She went home and prepped a holiday basket for her full of food and gifts."

That sounded exactly like something my mother would do, always thinking of others before herself.

Dad continued, "It was raining that night. Your mother told me to wait in the car, and she hurried over to the woman sitting here on the side of the road."

His finger tapped the background of the picture and I noticed for the first time how the downward strokes of paint gave the effect of pouring rain.

My dad became lost for a moment in the memory. I think he was beginning to realize, like me, that it felt better to embrace the thought of Mom instead of trying to push her away.

"Esther was a strange woman. I remember watching from a distance in the car. As she thanked your mother who was crouched down beside her, she reached for her and gently pressed her hand against Evelyn's stomach. They stood like that for the longest time. Strange, strange woman."

Just then Harrison came running in the back door. He had dirt smeared on his right cheek and sweat soaked the hair by his temples. He looked at me then ran and whispered something into Dad's ear.

"I'll go and change," Dad told him and picked up his glass of water.

Harrison looked at me again with a frown and ran back out the door. Dad left me alone at the table and walked back to his room.

I struggled to pull the pieces together. I flipped over the painting and looked at the date again. I pictured Esther placing her hand on my mother's stomach. My mind triggered the memory of the red poppy shriveling up in her hand.

"We can choose to give or take life from others," her voice echoed in my mind. My imagination pictured energy flowing from her hand into my mother.

I pondered my memory of Mom sitting next to me at the table explaining how long it took before she became a mother. *"We tried everything to start a family, but there isn't much a woman can do to get pregnant with lifeless ovaries."*

"Before I was born . . ." I whispered to myself. I placed my hand on my stomach as if I were there the night Mom delivered the basket in the pouring rain. My hand cupped the lower section of my gut, and I visualized what it was like being pregnant, feeling life inside of me.

She is the reason I'm alive, I realized. Esther had allowed my mother to create life and had healed her infertility. I wouldn't be here if Esther hadn't transferred part of her life's energy to my mother.

Dad walked back into the kitchen, showered and dressed. "I just called Dr. White. I'm taking Beck into the vet to find out what's wrong with her." He yelled for Harrison, "Harris, get your coat!"

Out the window I could see Beck's chin resting on the steps of the porch. Her dark eyes stared blankly off in the distance. I figured it must have been just her missing Mom, but Harrison must have been overly concerned.

I watched as Dad carried Beck into the backseat of the car. He was right. She didn't look well at all. Harrison climbed in after her and held her head gently in his lap as she shivered.

As Dad shut the door, he waved back to me in the

house, then hopped in the car and drove away.

I took the painting back upstairs and remembered my original objective of the late afternoon and climbed into my bed.

Chapter 21

Hours passed and the orange light of the sun slowly slipped out of my room, replacing itself with the darkness of the late evening.

My laptop began to ring with a bright blue message. Merritt waited on the other end, inviting me to video chat. I had avoided everyone for days, wanting to be alone, but reading his name on the screen gave me a sense of comfort, and I realized how much I had missed his company.

Before answering, I glanced in the mirror beside me. I looked awful. I couldn't remember how long it had been since I'd taken a shower. Reminding myself that Merritt cared for me enough to look past my dreadful appearance, I ignored the reflection and switched on my webcam.

Seeing his welcoming face as I answered his call felt like the warm embrace of a long lost friend. My heart felt sore from unhappiness and soaked into the positive emotion like a hot bubble bath.

"Hi," he spoke softly. I could see him hesitantly showing his cheerfulness to be sensitive to how I was feeling.

"My mom took a trip to Portland today and I'm just going crazy here alone missing you."

"I've missed you too," I said back. He smiled in relief.

I think being apart had been hard on him, but he had tried to give me space since the funeral.

The light of the computer screen lit up his face in the dark room and reflected against the bottom of his sparkling eyes. He pulled back the hood of his sweatshirt and shook out his wavy hair.

"How have you been feeling?" he asked.

I swallowed hard. The question shattered a glass sheet of emotions inside of me and brought back the reality of how my life will forever be different without Mom. I looked to the side and cupped my hand against my neck, feeling its tingling warmth.

"I'm okay," I lied.

I fidgeted with the stapler beside my computer. It slipped out of my hand and the noise of it hitting the desk made me jump in my seat. I tried laughing to hide my pain.

"I don't know, Merritt," I continued, "I'm scared . . ." I began feeling tears fill under my eyelids.

Mom was just the beginning. I was afraid of Nathaniel. Until I agreed to help him with whatever it was he wanted from me, he would never stop taking away the ones I loved.

"Rylee," he quickly replied. "I'm not going anywhere. You have your dad and your brother . . ."

"No, you don't understand!" I interrupted. "He's coming back. He won't stop until he's hurt everyone around me!"

"Who's coming back? What are you talking about?"

"Merritt, there's something I still haven't told you." I took a deep breath, ready to share what had really happened to my mother.

Suddenly, I noticed a silhouette shift in the moonlight behind Merritt.

I moved in closer to the computer screen and focused on the unclear pixels of his webcam display.

I watched as a shadowed figure slowly crept closer and closer to Merritt. As the distorted dark colors of the room morphed around the shadow, I recognized the round, familiar skull.

Nathaniel.

"Merritt! He's there! He's right behind you!" I yelled.

Merritt quickly turned, knocking the computer over so it fell to the ground. As it hit the floor our chat session disconnected.

"Merritt!" I screamed.

Without a moment to think I jumped out of my chair, knocking it over and bolted out of the room. I leapt down the stairs scrambling over Harrison's clutter of toys and sprinted outside.

Every muscle pumped thick with flowing adrenaline as I ran and cut through the woods straight for Merritt's home. My feet bounded, one in front of the other, as I ducked branches and avoided the disfigured roots of tree trunks rippling over the ground's surface. Tight air funneled through my lungs and sweat dripped off my face.

Through the thick trees I could see his yellow porch light flicker by the backside of his house. I pushed my body harder to pick up speed. In strides, I bounded up the steps and furiously knocked on the screen door.

"Merritt! Merritt! Open the door!" No answer. I grabbed the handle to see if it was unlocked, but it wouldn't budge.

I hit the door with my palms in anger and sprinted to the front of the house. My legs hurdled over the bushes that bordered the sides of his porch. Pounding with my fist, I called from the front door. There was no way to get inside.

"Merritt! Mrs. Emerson!" I searched the driveway for his mom's car and remembered him saying she had gone to the city. It was the perfect opportunity for Nathaniel.

Frustrated, I pushed my sweaty hair back that clung to the sides of my face and looked up at the dark, closed windows. It looked as if the house was empty from the outside.

Pacing in panic, I suddenly felt movement in my pocket and realized I had my cell phone with me. I pulled it out to find a text from Merritt. I exhaled a sigh of relief, overjoyed, until I read the written message.

"Come and find us."

They weren't at the house.

Included in the text were GPS coordinates. I plugged them into my phone and examined the map. The tracking numbers led a few acres away from the cemetery. I was horrified. *He has Merritt. What will he do to him?*

Anxiety swept over me. I tried to calm my nerves and searched around me for answers of what to do next.

"Ok, Rylee. Please, think. You have to think!"

Behind me in the driveway was Merritt's pickup truck. I stumbled over and crawled under the back tire, reaching for the spare key I had watched Merritt uncover once before.

I reached up and felt around the greasy machinery until I touched a magnetic box clinging to the inside of a small opening. I pulled out the key and climbed into the truck, trying to remember everything Merritt had taught me about driving stick.

"Okay, set it in reverse, start on the gas, ease the clutch," I mumbled to myself as the truck jerked and began speeding its way out of the driveway. My hands shook as I struggled to change gears and follow the map coordinates.

The street curved and split through the trees. As I hurried down the road I was surrounded by the shadows of the tall wall of wilderness. The bright light from the truck touched the pine branches that reached for me as I passed by. Blankets of cool droplets coated the side mirrors in damp dew.

The coordinates led me to an unfamiliar abandoned road. A light fog dressed the air and broke apart as I quickly sped through the veiled curtain of mist. The pickup violently shook over the uneven rocks and rattled loudly while driving over the bumpy trail.

My eyes scanned the shapes of the gravel path and tumbling weeds that flew by the windshield, until a strange figure grew in the center of the road.

A shriek escaped my throat as I slammed on the brakes and jerked the steering wheel. The truck came to a skidding halt on the shoulder of the road avoiding a collision with the uncertain figure.

I sat in shock as the headlights shone on the hermit standing still in the middle of the path.

She waited in the road, blocking me from progressing further. I jumped out of the truck and slammed the door behind me.

"Why are you here?! Have you been helping Nathaniel all along?" I screamed.

As I approached her, she stood still in silence. Her visionless eyes gazed in concern.

"My brother and I are no longer a part of each other's lives. I am here to voice a warning before you face this man," she spoke in her calm, raspy voice. "Whatever he tries to persuade you to do, know he only wants you for his own benefit."

"Why should I believe you?" I interrupted.

There was sadness in her expression. Her chin began

to weakly tremble almost as if she were ready to weep. I knew I had hurt her once before with my insensitive words, and I could see that my unbroken grudge continued to upset her. The words that next escaped her lips were so soft, yet so full of passion.

"What does your heart tell you?"

I recalled my father's story of that night in the rain. In my mind I pictured her connection as she stretched out her hand to heal my mom. She felt compassion toward my mother in the same way my mother felt pity for her.

I closed my eyes to dissect the feelings plastered inside my heart. Why did I desire to blame her for my mother's death? This woman had done nothing but help me and guide me. And I wouldn't be here except for her kindness years and years ago.

I opened my eyes again. Esther was small, fragile, and innocent. Searching past her frightful appearance, I could see the beautiful young woman with long, blond braids who had once journeyed through the jungle.

"I trust you, Esther," I whispered. She had no look of surprise as I said her name. Like always, I felt she was one step ahead of me and seemed to be aware of everything I already knew.

"Then you must end this now," she said. I could sense the urgency in her tone.

"How do I end it?"

There had to be a way to stop him so he couldn't hurt anyone else. But how do you take away a man's immortality? No matter what happened, he could still come back and haunt me for the rest of time. There had to be something I could do, something that no one else was capable of.

Then a thought entered my mind that I hadn't considered before. My heart dropped deep into an ocean of dread.

I looked at Esther and choked out the question, "There's only one way to stop him, isn't there?"

She nodded her head, and I knew what I had to do.

Esther stepped off of the pathway and motioned in the direction that I needed to go. A little trail trickled through the darkness into the forest and out of sight. I followed her pointed instruction and looked back. She had disappeared once more.

I began making my way down the dark path, terrified by the shadows and unfamiliar surroundings. Nathaniel could be anywhere watching. I had never in my life felt so in danger and so alone.

I was caught by the sounds of a faint moaning of pain off in the distance and recognized the source immediately.

"Merritt!" I yelled.

Chapter 22

I ran through the trees, breaking through the thick branches. The twigs and dry needles scratched and cut my arms. I stumbled and fell over a large fallen juniper trunk and rolled out into a clearing. My eyes fought to adjust to the light of the night sky.

Nathaniel stood tall across from me in the distance. His hairless head had a matted shine in the clear moonlight. I noticed for the first time the similarities in mannerisms he shared with his sister as he stood silently and watched me.

His hands patiently rocked, clasped behind his back, waiting for my arrival. In front of him I recognized the dark hood of Merritt's sweatshirt covering his head as he weakly sat tied to a wooden chair.

"So nice of you to join us, Rylee. Merritt and I have just been getting to know one another." He placed his hand on Merritt's shoulder, and I watched as he slowly began draining Merritt's energy. Merritt sunk lower and lower in his seat.

"Stop it!" I screamed. "It's me you want. You don't have to hurt him!"

Nathaniel hesitated before letting go and took a gradual step back.

"Walk with me?" he said and slowly stepped away from the chair. He turned and headed down another narrow trail hidden in the trees.

I looked back over at Merritt, struggling to keep his head up. My heart ached as I watched him tremble in his seat.

"He'll be fine," Nathaniel assured me.

Doing whatever it took to keep him away from Merritt, I cautiously followed as he led me out of the woods. As we climbed above a nearby turf I began to recognize my surroundings and realized we were heading directly toward the cemetery.

I stepped carefully and checked my footing as we passed over a rusty set of railroad tracks and onto the grassy hillside of haunting gravestones. We made our way through the rows of memorials when Nathaniel stopped at a specific stone.

I struggled to inhale as we neared the grave of my mother. Every step I took became heavier as I approached the tangible evidence that the world had snatched one of the most cherished elements from my life.

I hadn't been back since the funeral, and seeing the earth covering where she lay filled me with claustrophobic hysteria. The muscles quickly tightened in my face to hide any appearance of suffering. I looked away from Nathaniel and forced my body not to shudder.

"It really is a pity she had to go so soon. She could have had a few more lasting memories if you had listened to me in the beginning."

I swallowed deeply and forced tears from forming in my eyes. He might try to influence me through my emotions, but I wouldn't allow him to catch me vulnerable. I brushed his comment aside.

"I lost my mother too, Rylee," he spoke without

turning to face me, constantly focused on Mom's grave. "It was pneumonia. A cruel sickness. I understand the guilt of seeing someone important to you struggle to live and all you can do is sit there and watch the torment. It's torture to be filled with such power and be unable to use it."

If he was mentioning this to seek pity, he would have to find it somewhere else. Although my heart was hardened toward Nathaniel, I did feel a moment of sadness for his sister. It must have been hard on Esther losing her mother long ago.

"Why couldn't you save her? Surely you weren't selfish enough to hoard your power from your own mother."

The corner of Nathaniel's eye slightly twitched, but nothing else broke his facial surface showing weakness from my cutting words.

"It all goes back to Eve's curse," he explained. "It's some sort of block we have between our mothers. In the beginning, even Adam's son, Seth, tried using his echoing to save his mother from old age."

Echoing.

Shock flooded over me. Did he mean what I thought he meant?

"Oh, you didn't think you were the only balancer, did you?" He chuckled under his breath. "I've seen it. In the mirror. Back when my sister and I first found it, I would watch through the black stone ancient memories of her combing her pure, white hair as she gazed into the reflection. She really was the most beautiful woman I ever laid eyes on. And I've been around for a *long* time."

"Who are you talking about?"

"Eve, child. Back in the garden. Adam carved the mirror of onyx as a gift for his lovely wife. But when they were cast out it was left behind and locked away with the Tree of Life."

A tiny piece of me longed to see the mirror again. It was an ache I suppose all who looked into it shared as well. My imagination opened and I pictured Adam taking Eve by the hand and running from the garden. Perhaps she turned back for just a moment, torn to leave the gift she cherished so fondly behind.

"But the pool. Esther found it in the water . . ."

"She's shown you the wall, hasn't she? Remember the symbol burnt into its doorway? Only a balancer can unlock the opening. I saw this in the mirror too. It was Seth who first had the gift to pass the border and enter the garden."

I wasn't alone. There was another like me in the past. And even greater than that, I was capable of unlock the most ancient doorway in all of history. I could open the gateway Nathaniel had spent his entire life trying to get past.

"That's why I need you, Rylee. Don't you see? I must go back. And I have finally found the only person who can lead me to the tree." There was desperation hidden in his voice. Madness lingered in his countenance and I imagined he would destroy anything in his path to get what he wanted.

"Why would I help you?" I asked.

"I don't think you have much of a choice. Unless you enjoy losing people you love. I'm around forever, remember? You can never be rid of me."

As he spoke, the faint sound of a train whistle echoed in the distance. I stepped forward, so we were side by side. I knew, unless I decided to help him, he would try and serve as my personal cockroach, haunting me for the rest of my life.

"Will you leave Merritt alone? And my family?" I asked.

"We can disappear without a trace, and I will never come near them again." Nathaniel sighed a deep breath before his next words. "You were born for this purpose, Rylee. This is what you were meant for, helping me find the tree."

I squatted down and traced the words in my mother's stone. Although my back was turned to him, I knew he wouldn't try to harm me. Otherwise he'd just be harming himself.

I looked up and across the tracks in the shadows of the bushes and suddenly saw Esther watching from a distance. Her expression looked as if she were urging me to see something.

As my fingers stenciled the bottom of the stone, I suddenly felt a sharp fragment of onyx rock. It was a shattered piece of the black mirror from that first day we met. She must have visited here earlier and placed it by the gravestone.

As I looked into its reflecting image, I turned the angle once again to see a figure standing behind my shoulder, peering down at me. But it wasn't Nathaniel this time. This was someone I had never seen before. His thick locks hung low at his shoulders and he wore a handmade cover of roped grass and tree bark. There was a strange connection to this man unlike anything I had ever felt in my life.

Is this Seth? The other balancer from so long ago?

He looked at me with an expression of concern as if his eyes were pleading with me. Behind him was the wall to the garden Esther had shown me in the vision from her youth. He was guarding it.

A sudden instinct to protect the doorway weighed down on my senses. I could feel my echoing power churning through my insides. The decision was made. I could never let Nathaniel get what he wanted.

"You were born for *this* purpose," I whispered to myself.

Nathaniel took a step closer. "So, you've made up your mind then?"

My hand tightened. With all my might, I turned to the side and dug the jagged edge of black mirror into his calf, piercing the skin and the lower portion of muscle. He screamed and collapsed beside me.

I sprang up and began to run but tripped on a hidden gravestone. Pain shot up my leg as I fell forward, rolling down the steep hillside. When I finally stopped rolling I began to feel nauseated. My vision started to blur, and I worried for a moment that the pain in my ankle might cause me to black out.

As badly as it hurt, I had been expecting an injury to quickly occur and echo back to me after harming Nathaniel.

Looking up the hill, I spotted him as he tried pulling the rock from his leg. He groaned, and his face turned bright red in fury.

I crawled to a tall gravestone and ducked behind it before he had a chance to look up. Stopping myself from crying out, I squeezed my ankle, hoping the pressure would distract me from the pain.

In the distance I began to hear the rumbling train making its way closer and looked up to see its bright headlight a mile down the track.

I could hear Nathaniel's off beat steps as he limped his way through the gravestones, moaning as he searched for me.

"I know you're hurt too, Rylee! You can't get away from me," he shouted.

My fingers stumbled through the dead grass and scratched against a small, prickled pinecone. I reached out for it and chucked it away from me. The sound of it bouncing against a distant tree distracted Nathaniel, and he changed direction.

As he stumbled away, the approaching locomotive whistled again. The piercing sound scraped at my eardrums, and I could almost feel the ground shaking from its heavy, rolling wheels.

I pushed off beneath me with all my might and hopped toward the tracks, avoiding the use of my hurt ankle. Nathaniel turned back to see me running and hobbled as fast as his injured leg would allow him to go.

I calculated the speed of the oncoming train, bolting as it approached faster and faster. My blood rushed cold as I realized my chances of crossing in time were slim. I switched off the feeling of pain in my ankle and psychologically forced it to numb.

My strides became longer as my arms pulled me, crossing fiercely at my sides. At the last possible second, I leaped across the tracks in front of the train and crossed to the other side as it thundered dangerously behind me.

I stumbled to the ground and picked myself back up focused on reaching Merritt. I was grateful for the head start the long train granted me while Nathaniel waited, delayed on the other side of the tracks. Depending on the length, it could give me two or three extra minutes to reach him.

I followed the pathway that led back into the woods and came upon Merritt, still tangled in ropes around the wooden chair. I lost my footing as sharp pain attacked my ankle again, causing me to slide to the ground by Merritt's feet. I crept the rest of the way determined to save him before Nathaniel had a chance to get back.

"I'm getting you out of here, Merritt. Hold on." My fingers shook and fretted as they frantically tried untying the knots to free him. Merritt struggled to come to his senses.

"Rylee . . . Rylee," he repeated. He looked exhausted as sweat poured down the sides of his soaking face. Suddenly, he leaned forward and blacked out against my shoulder.

As he collapsed into me, I heard uneven footsteps quickly approaching and knew Nathaniel was returning. Merritt was so heavy and I only had seconds to decide what to do before he came back.

I couldn't let him see me. I looked over my shoulder and found a fallen tree with a gap large enough for a body to hide underneath.

"Ryyyyyy-lee," I heard Nathaniel taunt me as he walked through the trees like we were children playing an innocent game of hide and seek.

He limped back into the meadow and scanned the quiet setting. Disappointment clearly showed in his face when he saw no sign of me anywhere, just a slumped over hooded body tied to the chair, almost loose enough to escape and slip away.

"That's a shame," he said as he glanced down pitifully, knowing I hadn't had enough time to untie Merritt and run. I listened closely as he circled the wooden chair.

"Is this what you want, Rylee? To keep hiding while I slowly kill off your loved ones, one by one? After him, what about little Harrison? Shall I come for him next?"

My heart punched against my chest. I tried to control and steady my breathing, so the sound of fear escaping my mouth wouldn't give me away.

He lifted his hand beside the chair and paused, waiting and hoping I would jump out of the darkness, but I kept silent.

"Last chance," he sang.

Merritt slowly regained consciousness and looked around, recognizing his surroundings. *Stay put*, I thought to myself. I slightly raised my head, knowing this may be my last opportunity to see Merritt. Then I held my breath.

Grabbing the shoulder of the hooded sweatshirt, Nathaniel clawed his fingers deep in and intensely began soaking up life with all his might. I closed my eyes and forced myself not to scream.

The chair fell on its side and he continued stealing life until there was none left to take, and it was too late. *Goodbye, Merritt,* I thought to myself. There was no hope. All that was left were a few last, desperate breaths clinging to that tiny flame of life before it blew out.

Chapter 23

Nooo!" Merritt screamed and quickly climbed out from under the tree trunk. Nathaniel jerked his head up. His eyes widened in disbelief as he watched Merritt running toward him in the distance. He looked down at the lifeless body and frantically lifted the sweatshirt hood.

I lied on the ground sideways in the chair with only a few breaths left, between life and death. Staring back up at him, I met his puzzled gaze. I had switched places with Merritt and outwitted Nathaniel. Had he just looked under the hood, he would have realized I was right beside him the whole time.

"You can't hurt anyone anymore, Nathaniel." The words choked out of my throat. This was the only way to stop him. If he killed me, my gift of balancing would in turn kill him. I felt my energy exhale out of my soul and attack in his direction.

He suddenly dropped to the ground and began gasping for air as his strength slowly melted away. I watched him twitch and shiver on the ground for a moment, then go hauntingly still.

Then all went silent.

I felt no emotion. All that was left was the knowledge of existence. I floated into emptiness. Every limb of my body became buoyant against the law of gravity and floated into an ocean of nothingness.

Somewhere, but nowhere at the same time, for there was no sense of direction or being, no left or right, backward or forward, but somewhere cracked a glow of warm light, and it gently flooded over me.

I was standing on a long stretch of road. I recognized it from my dreams. Above me, the glowing moon and stars welcomed my innocent presence. The coolness of peace swept past my broken down heart.

"Rylee!" I turned around in search of the caller shouting my name.

"Rylee!" It echoed in a sad state of panic. I recognized the familiar voice of Merritt. Down the road I saw him, or I should say his shape, kneeling on the ground with his back turned toward me. He was a radiating energy, the way Esther could see the shapes of individuals around her. I ran for him.

Like in a state of dreaming, the faster I ran, the slower I became, and the longer it took to reach him. I passed Nathaniel lying on the side of the road lifeless. There was no color emitting from his form. The rocks and the trees surrounding him glowed with more life than he did. He was gone.

I finally caught up to Merritt who was huddled over a motionless body on the ground. I leaned over his shoulder and recognized the strange energy dimly lit inside the girl he was holding. It was me. I was watching myself die.

I could feel the ache and worry in Merritt's heart, as if there was a direct channel translating his emotions straight into my understanding. *Don't go, Ry. Don't leave me.* In his eyes I saw his fear, a deep, unbearable fear that he wouldn't be able to exist if I were gone. I understood exactly what he was feeling. And my heart burned for his sorrow.

Suddenly, I heard my name again, but coming from a different direction. The source was another familiar voice I recognized, this time much calmer.

I turned and saw her standing there, so young and beautiful, smiling back at me.

"Mom."

I hurried toward her and collapsed into her warm embrace, burying my head deep into her shoulder.

"What's going on, Mom? What will happen to Merritt?" I cried.

"Rylee, the balance of everything is so beautiful. It all makes sense. It ties together into one solid matter that we can't understand in this life. But it is absolutely glorious." She pulled away and brushed the hair out of my face, then leaned in and whispered in my ear, "Close your eyes."

I felt her hands brush against my eyelashes and wrap around my face.

She began to show me a story, the way Esther could when she covered my eyes. I was flooded and surrounded by memories of my past, encompassed in a strange vertigo of life events spinning around me like a carousel. Although they flickered by and dissolved at instant speed, I absorbed every detail.

I was kissing Merritt and blasting music with Mom in the car. There were glimpses of birthday parties, and elementary school teachers, fights on the playground, and learning to ride my bicycle. I made snow angels, cart wheeled through sprinklers, chased butterflies, and crashed into piles of crunchy, autumn leaves. They continued backwards reaching deeper and deeper into my past.

I was suddenly in a hospital room. The atmosphere was full of panic and fear. I turned to the side and in a nearby hospital bed saw my mother screaming, surrounded by a herd of doctors and nurses. I could feel her unbearable suffering.

I wanted to push through the bubbled cloud of blue scrubs to save her. Her screaming and groaning was suddenly overpowered by an unfamiliar noise, a high-pitched squeal coming from a different source.

I looked over to see the doctor hold up a tiny baby with thick, dark hair. Her eyes closed tightly as she cried with all the trembling strength she had inside of her.

The doctor quickly reached up and set her in mother's arms, who then kissed the baby's head and rested the infant against her chest, holding her closely, never wanting to let go.

All of the pain I had ever experienced completely evaporated in a single instant and replaced itself with joy and a feeling of pure love. It soaked into parts of me I never knew existed. I felt a bonding connection of care, hope, and affection stronger than the touch of solid matter and more real than anything I had ever known.

This was the moment I was born. I felt the beauty of balance my mother was trying to explain. The joy that filled the room the day I entered the world matched the sorrow of those left behind as I lay lifeless in Merritt's arms at the end of my existing journey.

Everything balanced. Everything had its opposite. The deep pains of life were healed with sprinkles of rich happiness. Everything we experienced had a significant purpose.

I opened my eyes and stood again with my mother, overlooking my Imminent death. I had not noticed before that beside Merritt stood the hermit.

Her colors of energy glimmered. She gazed in our direction, and I could sense her sight was no longer clouded. She looked straight at me and studied the features of my face that she was never able to witness before.

She stood up and walked toward my mother and me.

"She made a sacrifice," she said. "The actions of the balancer must be returned."

Reaching out, she placed her hand against my ribcage over the heart of my body lying on the ground.

"I will take your place," she whispered. "You are still needed here."

I watched as the shining power inside her quickly funneled from her hand and into my lifeless body in Merritt's arms. I felt a tingling sensation and an instinct to reconnect my spirit with the corpse on the ground. The urgency pulled at me, making it almost unbearable to stay still.

"Mom, I can't leave you," I cried. She reached down and held my hand, placing the other on my cheek.

"I am right here. I'm not going anywhere. You won't see me or hear me." She placed my hand on my heart. "But through here, you can always feel that I'm near."

I hugged her as tightly as I could. She kept whispering in my ear, "I'm right here, Rylee."

I suddenly lost all my energy and went limp in her arms. Her voice began to alter into a deeper tone, "I'm right here, Rylee. I'm right here. Wake up, Rylee!"

I opened my eyes and found myself pressed against Merritt's chest. My entire body began to ache and I felt the coldness of the air around me.

"Where's Mom?" I asked him.

"Rylee, you're alive!" He pulled me in closer and hugged me without letting go. I realized that I had come back into my body where Nathaniel had left me.

The devastation of losing Mom again quickly melted away in Merritt's arms. I knew everything would be all right, and we were now safe. He was here and holding me, protecting me.

My fingers clutched his sleeve, and my breath warmed my face, insulated in his cotton shirt. I held him like a frightened child clung to their parents' arms.

I turned from Merritt and felt a lifeless body beside me. Esther.

She was lying on her side looking over at me. The whiteness in her eyes had faded away and for the first time, I was able to see her natural eye color. They were the same bright blue as her brother's.

Just like when I had held my mother in my arms the night she had died, I could sense that Esther was gone. Although her spirit had left her, she looked at peace.

A distance away, Nathaniel's body was sprawled across the ground. We watched as he slowly began to shrivel into dust, like the flower I had witnessed in Esther's hand days before. In time nothing remained of him, not even his old jacket or leather shoes. He faded away into nothing, blending into the Earth with his particles of remains.

I turned back to Esther, and she was gone.

Chapter 24

We drove Merritt's truck up my driveway and saw my dad's car parked outside. I remembered how they had left to take Beck to the doctor and hoped everything was all right. I wasn't sure if Harrison could handle another death so soon.

Merritt jumped out and walked around the truck to open my door. He reached for my hand and gently helped me out of the seat. My strength was slowly returning, but I cautiously leaned on his shoulder for support.

As I began to walk toward the house, Merritt stood still with my fingers still closed in his hands. He softly pulled me back in and wrapped his arms around me.

I leaned my head against his chest and soaked in his warmth. My body exhaled deep relief knowing how close we had come to losing each other tonight.

"I love you so much, Rylee," he spoke softly. I pulled my head back and rested my hands on the sides of his face.

"I love you." The words felt too simple. There was no way of describing how I would give up everything for him or how my spirit longed to be entwined with his for all eternity.

My lips pressed to his, hoping my touch would show

him a glimpse of what he meant to me. I wanted to transfer the energy of warmth back and push out all of the kindness he had shown me, echoing back to him.

I looked up into his dark eyes and whispered, "You are . . . You're my everything, Merritt."

He smiled and began leading me back into the house. I limped cautiously to avoid putting weight on my injured ankle as we climbed the stairs to the porch.

I opened the door and led him in behind me. The house felt quiet and still.

Suddenly, Harrison appeared from around the corner with a bright smile stretched across his face.

"Hurry, sissy, come and see Beck!" He grabbed my hand and led us into the family room. Dad was lying on the ground next to Beck by the fire. The flames crackled in the background and lit up the walls with capturing warmth of the yellow glow.

Beck was fast asleep, curled up on top of Mom's blue, checkered blanket. As we came closer, Harrison hurried around to the other side of Beck.

Beside her was a small litter of white and caramel puppies. They were tangled together into an adorable collection of light covered fuzz.

We knelt down beside them and Harrison lifted one up, setting it gently in Merritt's cupped hands. Beck opened her eyes and watched us with a pinch of cautiousness. I held on to Merritt's arm and leaned in close, studying the pup's tightly shut newborn eyes. Reaching out with a single finger, I gently stroked the wrinkled forehead between its brows.

I could sense its pure innocence and excitement for the beginning of life. This fresh feeling of starting over was contagious and began flowing inside of me.

I looked up at Dad who I could feel shared the joy of

this new beginning. The hidden smile in his eyes had for an instant forgotten the pain of losing my mother. I felt an emotion of security and began to realize we would all heal.

With time the pain would turn into more of a memory, and in her honor, we could begin to live again, the way she would have wanted us to.

The pavement was wet from the recently fallen rain and the sound of the flowing river nearby cleared my mind. In the distance I listened as a flock of honking geese soared in unison across the sky.

I held a fresh bouquet of bright yellow flowers and made my way to my mother's grave. Kneeling down, I felt the soothing flower petals between my dry fingers before placing it next to her stone.

I turned and looked back down the rows of graves in a different light than the day of the funeral. None of these gravesites were numbers that faded away into nothingness. I realized each and every deceased soul continued to affect our lives.

The flowers that decorated her grave were a symbol that her life was connected to others around her. Just like a memory, her existence lingered and though she was no longer tangible, she molded into the lives of loved ones and continued to exist through those she left behind.

I walked down a gravel pathway that led to the shore of the river. Light waves trickled in and out through the smooth pebbles resting beside the toes of my red shoes.

I reached into my jacket pocket and delicately pulled out a small poppy flower and set it in the shallow current. The water swept it away in a few brief seconds, and I watched as it floated out into the larger waves. The sacrifice of Esther became a permanent piece of me. Tilting my wrist to the side, I studied the blue and green veins painted down my arm. I could feel her life flowing through my blood stream and felt a special appreciation for the life she gave for me. She had become a part of who I was.

I folded my arms and closed my eyes to take in the sounds of the wind through the trees. Peace. I inhaled the fresh smell of rain and felt the heartaches of the past begin to heal.

Epilogue

Warm water soothed my shaking hands as I held them under the running faucet in the school bathroom. I patted my face and reached for the paper towel dispenser. When I glanced up at the mirror I tried looking past the face in front of me in search for the transformation that lied beneath over the last eventful months.

"Rylee, it's time," Shyler patiently called and entered the ladies' room. She walked up and placed her arms around my shoulders. "You're gonna be amazing tonight."

As she led me toward the doorway, my long, blue dress swayed with my footsteps, and the clicks of my heels echoed with the acoustics of the bathroom walls. My hair was pinned up into a waterfall of thick brown curls that poured down to one side.

I opened the door to find Merritt in black slacks and a button up blue shirt waiting to chaperone me backstage. Combed back and dried, Merritt's hair formed perfect waves that tucked neatly into place. He lifted his elbow to the side as an escorting invitation.

"I better go find my seat," Shyler said. She squeezed underneath my elbow and left the two of us alone.

Merritt smiled and stared in my direction as we made

our way down the empty, dark hallway of never-ending red lockers.

"What is it?" I asked.

"You look breathtaking."

I looked down and felt my cheeks beginning to blush.

"Well, you happen to look stunning yourself," I replied back and softly nudged him in the side.

As we reached the back door to the auditorium, he stopped and faced me. He leaned in and kissed my cheek. I stepped forward and wrapped my arms around him to bring him in closer.

"Your mom would be so proud of you," he whispered. The sudden thought of her made me smile.

Behind the door we began to hear a deep voice introducing the girl's choir.

"I better go," I whispered.

My arms slid down his sides and grabbed his hands. I held on for an extra moment then hurried to the stage.

Greeted by risers and rows of matching dark blue gowns, I walked past all of the girls and stood in front of the microphone at center stage. I stared up into the bright spotlight and felt the heat warm my skin. *This is for Mom*, I thought to myself.

As the piano keys began to fill the air with musical chords, I looked to the side stage curtain. In the shadows, I imagined her being there. I felt her fill my heart and knew a piece of her was with me. My mother was near, and she would hear me sing.

I filled my lungs deeply with air and let the melody glide past my lips and soak into the concert hall. The words danced off my tongue with grace and the accompanying background of blended female voices lifted the sound into a thick, rich dance of musical symmetry.

My mind flooded with flashes of memories and sparks

of emotions. I thought of Merritt, our childhood summers, and the kiss behind the waterfall. And how much I loved him.

I thought of my family, Harrison, and Dad. I pictured Shyler who had always been there for me, Esther who gave her life for me, and my mother.

With everything that had happened, with everything that still would happen, I knew I needed to live for her. I needed to let myself be happy and honor her by letting the joy of the world be recognized and overpower the bad. I was here for a reason, and I would live my life to its fullest potential.

As the song neared the end, our voices blended and churned like the imaginary honey pot. We became one voice with one purpose in our melody. The sound echoed through the hall, and I felt goose bumps begin to blossom on my arms.

The music opened my heart and allowed me to sense life in a more complete way. I could feel my mother wrap her arms around me in a loving embrace and I prayed she would never let go.

When the song came to an end, everyone soaked in the silence for a long moment. Then, in an instant, my eardrums rang with the sound of applause.

The concert continued on as choir after choir organized themselves on the stage and swayed to the sound of the music.

"Wasn't your sister great tonight?" Merritt leaned over and whispered to Harrison. He swatted at a buzzing honeybee that had somehow made its way inside the auditorium.

"Mmm-hmm," Harrison nodded as he looked down at the plastic cars in his lap. He rolled the tires over the armrests, up Merritt's shoulder, and crashed them into his leg with the whispered sounds of monstrous car explosions.

"I bet your mom would have loved to be here to see this."

Harrison stopped and smiled up at Merritt.

Quickly, Merritt head locked him in his arms and gave a little nudge. Then he transitioned through the serious moment by flicking Harrison right in the ear.

"Ouch," Harrison giggled and grabbed his ear. At that exact moment Merritt jumped in his seat and clutched the side of his face. The floating bee from earlier had landed on his ear and surprisingly gave him a minor sting.

Harrison could hardly keep his laughter in. "What goes around comes around," he whispered.

"Yeah, I guess so," Merritt said as he rubbed his stinging skin. Puzzled, he thought about the sudden coincidence of instant karma.

He watched as Harrison quietly pulled a tiny fragment of chipped off onyx rock out of his pocket and studied his face in the pocket-sized reflection.

Acknowledgments

My heart pours out in gratitude to all who have helped transform my dream into a reality:

To God, who reached and found the words inside of me that I didn't know existed. I owe Him everything.

Thank you to Mitchell, my best friend who supported me unwaveringly, even when I didn't believe in myself. And little Trekker, the sunshine in my life who makes me laugh everyday.

To my sweet family, who have been my wonderful cheerleaders and my inspiration for happiness. Love you Mom and Dad, Grandma and Grandpa, Adam, Kenny, and so, so many others! Shout out to my wonderful beta-reader sisters (and niece), Soonhee, Lydia, Lisa, and Ella, for helping my frumpy caterpillar of a story bloom into something less caterpillar-y.

I couldn't have done this without the help of everyone at Cedar Fort. Thank you for believing in my book and helping me grow.

A special thanks to my precious mother-in-law, Janice, for sparking my passion for writing. You had the faith that I could succeed and none of this would have happened if it weren't for you.

To everyone who writes and inspires me and others to do the same, and to my readers who make everything worth it, thanks for sharing my world.

About the Author

Jessica Blackburn currently lives in the beautiful Columbia Gorge with her family. When she's not spilling out her imagination into writing, Jessica spends her spare time blogging, snapping photos, waitressing, teaching Sunday School, and obsessing over her baby son and loving husband. During thunderstorms, you can find Jessica cuddled up in her puffed blanket with fuzzy socks and peppermint hot chocolate.